Praise for
Kristine Kathryn Rusch

"Rusch is a great storyteller."

—RT Book Reviews

"Whether [Rusch] writes high fantasy, horror, sf, or contemporary fantasy, I've always been fascinated by her ability to tell a story with that enviable gift of invisible prose. She's one of those very few writers whose style takes me right into the story—the words and pages disappear as the characters and their story swallows me whole….Rusch has style."

—Charles de Lint

"A masterful writer is at work."

—Orson Scott Card
New York Times bestselling author

"Rusch's greatest strength…is her ability to close down a story and leave the reader feeling that the author could not possibly have wrung any more satisfaction out of the piece."

—The Kansas City Star

"Rusch is a great storyteller—easily the equal of Patterson or Koontz."

—Analog

"Kristine Kathryn Rusch is one of the best writers in the field."

—SFRevu

"[Rusch's] writing style is simple but elegant, and her characterization excellent."

—Mark Morris
Beyond

"Like early Ray Bradbury, Rusch has the ability to switch on a universal dark."

—The London *Times*

"Kristine Kathryn Rusch's crime stories are exceptional, both in plot and in style."

—Ed Gorman
Mystery Scene Magazines

"[Rusch's] short fiction is golden."

—The Kansas City Star

Praise for the Retrieval Artist series

"If you love puzzle mysteries, crime novels, well-invented sci-fi worlds, or stories about characters you can believe in and care about, you owe it to yourself to give Rusch's Retrieval Artist novels a try."

—Orson Scott Card
New York Times bestselling author

"What links [Miles Flint] to his most memorable literary ancestors is his hard-won ability to perceive the complex nature of morality and live with the burden of his own inevitable failure."

—*Locus*

Praise for the Smokey Dalton series
(writing as Kris Nelscott)

"Nelscott's series setting, in the turbulent late '60s, gives her books layers of issues of racism, class, and war, all of which still seem to remain sadly timely today."

—*Oregonian*

"Nelscott has her own, very distinct voice, and her series creates its own deeply satisfying pleasures and cogent points."

—*Seattle Times*

"It's not hard to draw parallels between Nelscott's PI Smokey Dalton and Walter Mosley's Easy Rawlins, another secretive, canny black man trying to solve mysteries while circumspectly navigating the white world. But Dalton's no knock-off. (Would you label the hundreds of hard-boiled detectives who've appeared in Raymond Chandler's wake mere Marlow Xeroxes because they're white?)"

—*Entertainment Weekly*

Also by
Kristine Kathryn Rusch

The Retrieval Artist Series:

The Disappeared
Extremes
Consequences
Buried Deep
Paloma
Recovery Man
Duplicate Effort
Anniversary Day
Blowback

The Smokey Dalton Series (as Kris Nelscott):

A Dangerous Road
Smoke-Filled Rooms
Thin Walls
Stone Cribs
War at Home
Days of Rage

SANTA AND OTHER CHRISTMAS CRIMINALS

KRISTINE KATHRYN RUSCH

wMg
Publishing

Santa and Other Christmas Criminals

"Rehabilitation" by Kristine Kathryn Rusch was first published in *Ellery Queen's Mystery Magazine*, January, 2000.

"Snow Angels" by Kristine Kathryn Rusch was first published in *Alfred Hitchcock's Mystery Magazine*, January/February 2006.

"Doubting Thomas" by Kristine Kathryn Rusch was first published in *Villains Victorious*, edited by Martin H. Greenberg and John Helfers, Daw Books, 2001.

"Substitutions" by Kristine Kathryn Rusch was first published in *Places to Be, People to Kill*, edited by Martin H. Greenberg and Brittiany A. Koren, Daw Books, 2007.

"Nutball Season" by Kristine Kathryn Rusch was first published on the SciFi.com website, December 24, 2003.

WMG Publishing
www.wmgpublishing.com

Contents

Santa and Other Christmas Criminals

Kristine Kathryn Rusch

Introduction
Me & Santa

*L*ET ME SAY RIGHT OFF: Santa's been good to me. He always arrived on time. He ate the obligatory cookies, left some *awesome* presents, and managed to keep the mystique in Christmas longer than necessary. I met him on a few occasions, mostly in department stores, but once at a holiday party at the college where my father taught.

Santa even showed up at my neighbor's house the Sunday before Christmas. Santa walked in the front door and gave all the little kids in the room (including me) a present. He tracked in snow, and then with a few deep chuckles, he left.

We weren't allowed to watch him leave—we were told it would spook the reindeer. We were a bit concerned that Santa hadn't used the chimney, until someone (my friend's dad?) explained that the chimney led directly into the furnace, and sliding into the furnace just wasn't safe.

Clearly, my relationship with Santa has been a good one. So why do I write stories in which he's the villain?

Or if not the villain then a possibly shady (or insane) character? Maybe because he betrayed me.

The relationship every little kid has with Santa always ends in betrayal. He shows up, he promises magic, he *delivers* magic, and then—one day—someone says he's not real. And we're supposed to believe that.

Really, he's just moved on to other kids. Kids who are just a little more starry-eyed. Kids who are newer, fresher, *younger*. Who wouldn't feel betrayed?

Santa shows up in this collection three times. "Rehabilitation" follows the adventures of a mall Santa during the Christmas season that changes his life. "Doubting Thomas" explains the importance of chimneys, and why Santa does all of that sneaking around. And my personal favorite, "Nutball Season," harks back to *Miracle on 34th Street* which is, by far, the best Christmas movie ever made.

Criminals show up in every story, except the last one. Sometimes the criminals are a bit too broad to be believed, but sometimes they're truly scary. In "Snow Angels," the annual hunt for a Christmas tree turns dark. And in "Substitutions," Christmas Eve takes a decidedly sinister twist for a replacement worker on the dirtiest of dirty jobs.

So if you're a bit tired of the same old sappy Christmas tales, this collection is for you. And if you read every story contained herein, you might never look at the Jolly Old Elf in quite the same way again.

—*Kristine Kathryn Rusch*
Lincoln City, Oregon
November 23, 2010

Rehabilitation

THIS CHRISTMAS WAS DIFFERENT. For the first time in fifteen years, he had a choice of jobs. *Help Wanted* signs littered Portland. From restaurants to boutiques, from offices to museums, the red signs with the outlined white lettering beckoned from every window.

But Matt took the job he had taken every year since he started wandering. It still shocked him how quickly the malls hired their Santas, how little time these places, which entrusted other people's children to big men with appealing laughs, spent on researching their employees' backgrounds. When he had started in 1984, barely twenty and hardly large enough to play Santa, computers were rare things, personal data hard to trace. But it wasn't now, and lawsuits were more common. Sometimes he wondered how many of his colleagues in their red suits with fake white fur trim had records, and how many of them used the information they got from a tyke in ways that would have made the real Santa leave coal in their stockings.

He liked playing Santa; it was the only time he felt as if he had worth. Every year, he heard from the mall manager that he was the best Santa the mall had ever had, and every year he promised to return the next, and every year, he was somewhere else, with a different name, and a different story. It used to be that he would arrive in his new home with a different dream, but at thirty-five, he was getting too old for dreams. Dreams were a luxury a man like him should never indulge in.

His résumé said nothing about his real past, of course. This year's named him Matthew J. Sturtz, a man who had graduated from the University of Oregon with a Ph.D. in English, who had spent most of his years as a professor of English Literature at Gustavus Adolphus. He was taking a sabbatical, his résumé said, returning to his home state to write the definitive paper on Herman Melville's "Bartleby the Scrivener," and even though he had only been here a month, he already felt the need for a diversion, a way to interact with people, to get out now and then.

He had learned, over the years, that such unusual detail—along with the correct addresses and phone numbers—got him a long way in the Santa business. Most false names were common ones, easy to spell, so he always chose something like Sturtz. Most fake résumés were filled with jobs impossible to check, so he made his easy to check, out of state, and plausible, so plausible in fact that most personnel managers never bothered. When quizzed, he had his answers down so pat, that nothing surprised him.

He spent October studying Melville and "Bartleby"—he could discuss both with pedantic enthusiasm, guaranteed to make the interviewer's eyes glaze within thirty seconds.

If Matt did his job right—and he always did—the interviewer had no suspicions about him at all. If Matt did his job right, the interviewer would always end the interview with, "You're exactly the kind of man we want playing Santa. Please go downstairs. They'll brief you on everything you'll need."

The mall that hired him as one of this year's rotating Santas was one of the oldest in Portland. It had five anchor stores, two stories, and a new wing. An atrium, with a high-domed glass ceiling, in the center of the mall provided the space for his little kingdom: a throne-sized chair with two large cushions, a giant Christmas tree—real, he soon learned, with that wonderful fresh scent—and a pile of presents stacked beneath it, each marked with a child's sex and age, each donated by a different store.

This place had spent a lot of money on the costumes too: no fake white fluff that had pilled or grown gray with time. White fur instead—not real, of course, but the kind that covered the best stuffed animals. The suits were red velvet, the beards and wigs from a men's costume shop that guaranteed authenticity. When Matt applied the spirit gum, he felt as if he were going to go on stage instead of into the sunlit atrium with a gaggle of kids waiting to sit on his lap.

His first day, the day after Thanksgiving, went well, as did his second, and third. No baby peed on him, no frightened toddler kicked him in the wrong place, no angry parent returned demanding a different present for his precious little darling. Each night, Matt returned to home—one of the hotels near the airport that catered to out-of-towners who rented by the week—put his feet up on the presswood coffee table, feeling as if he'd had real human contact, as if things—for this one brief instant— were good once again.

He knew it was an illusion, and that come December 25th, the illusion would evaporate as if it had never been. Matt Sturtz would become someone else, would live somewhere else, and gradually lose the comfort the season had given him.

He knew all that, and he no longer minded. It was the rhythm of his life, the only tradition he had, and he valued it, above all else.

***

ON TUESDAY, DECEMBER FIRST, the rain came down in sheets, and the bus driver, obviously new, struggled to keep the Metro on the slick roads. Drivers honked and cursed, pedestrians stood away from the curbs to keep from getting splashed, and Matt had to walk the last three blocks to make sure he was on time to work.

In the locker room, the previous Santa was hanging up his uniform. He was an older man, a grandfather or so he said, who loved spending time with children. He grinned when he saw Matt close the filthy metal door and grab the handle of the dented locker the mall had provided him and his precious suit.

"Not a lot of business," the grandfather said, "but I'll bet it'll pick up tonight."

"It usually does," Matt said, and then turned his back as he pulled off his jeans. Some of the Santas wore their jeans under the suit, but the kids could always see that. By the time he had finished changing, the grandfather was gone.

Matt applied his beard, mustache and wig, always amazed that with the right facial hair, he could look forty years older than he really was. He practiced the eye twinkle in the scratched mirror above the sink, then put on his cap, and let himself out of the locker room.

Here, in the mall proper, he was Santa. He walked with a joy he never had anywhere else. He smiled at children, and ho-ho-ho-ed on command. As he made his way past the decorated fake trees in the center of the mall, past the women with strollers, the men looking harried, he assisted in little ways. He helped catch a two-year-old who was on a shrieking, giggling tear away from her father who was trying to adjust the infant he carried in a neck sling. As the man tried to express his gratitude, Matt moved on. He caught a package that an overloaded business woman dropped, and then he was at his location.

The piped-in music in this part of the mall had class; Frank Sinatra singing "Have Yourself a Merry Little Christmas" which, Matt knew, would be followed by Ella

Fitzgerald wondering "What Are You Doing New Year's Eve?" He appreciated that. There were only so many Muzak renditions of "Jingle Bells" that a man could experience in one lifetime.

The throne was comfortable, and the elf, a middle-aged librarian with a knack for keeping people in line, grinned at him as he settled in. There was no line at the moment: there probably wouldn't be until parents got off work—most of the stay-at-home parents were preparing dinner—and it was too early for the last-minute shoppers to crowd the mall. He had an hour or more to keep himself occupied before the first real busy session started.

From the throne, he could see the nearby stores: the Lord & Taylor anchor store with its male and female dummies wearing Christmas evening wear, gold garlands around the windows, and expensive gifts under a very real, very large tree; the Musicland beside it, the window garish with red and green and white peppermint paper; the Waldenbooks on the other side, its display filled with coffee-table books that people would look at once and then never touch again.

He imagined having a gift list, shopping, as so many men did now, hurrying from his 9 to 5 for an hour at the mall before stopping for take-out Chinese on the way home. He wondered if he would have been that kind of husband, that sort of father, the one who was involved, who wore a baby in a sling around his neck while chasing a joyful toddler. He wondered and felt the familiar twist in his heart, and then made himself think of something else.

If he turned ever so slightly in the throne, he could see the stores with the outdoor access: the photographer on the corner, advertising family portraits; the jeweler who specialized in diamonds and easy credit; the beauty shop that also did nails. They were empty as well.

He suppressed a sigh and the elf grinned at him. It was an infectious grin with its own twinkle, and it made him wonder if she felt discriminated against, if she thought she could be as good—or better—a Santa than he could.

He smiled back, then glanced at the double doors at the other side of the anchor store. Cars were cruising the rain-soaked parking lot. A van with bald tires screeched so loudly as it stopped that it nearly drowned out Ella. The man who got out of the passenger's side was little more than a boy, really, a teenager who had gotten his height, but hadn't gotten rid of the lanky gawkiness that marked him as a stranger in his newer bigger body. He pulled his battered leather jacket around him as he ran into the jewelry store, pausing to look at the engagement rings in the display beside the window, before going in where Matt could no longer see him.

Getting engaged at Christmas. All the hopes and dreams and special moments tied together. The twist again, so fierce that he had to turn away. He faced the main section of the mall, saw the father he had rescued, the baby now asleep against his chest, the little girl pointing at the tree. The father grinned at Matt, Matt grinned back, and suddenly, he was in business.

***

IT WAS AS IF THE MAGIC held him in those hours, the heart-warming magic found only in hour-long T.V. shows and the annual holiday Disney movies. He could believe that each child who sat on his lap would go home to a large tree, with ample presents beneath, loving parents, a new year destined to be filled with only joy. The grubby hands pulling on his beard, the candy-soured breath, whispering important secrets that usually showed the triumph of marketing in the American psyche, somehow gave him reassurance that in other homes, at least, something wonderful was happening, something he could share for a brief moment, and that, he assured himself, was enough.

Matt always insisted on telling his elf the child's wishes so that the elf could tell the parents when she handed out the present; that way he had done his duty as only Santa could. The hours went quickly, the eager faces blurred, and when the line finally dwindled to nothing, he felt a healthy exhaustion that he never got when he worked construction or got the odd bartending job.

He leaned back in his throne, glanced at his watch, and saw he had fifteen minutes until the mall closed.

"You didn't even take a break," his elf said. "I suppose you could now. I doubt we'll get anyone else."

In his mind's eye, he saw an imaginary tow-headed boy, dragging his tired mother through the large mall, only to arrive at Santa's Village to find Santa's throne empty.

He smiled. "I can last fifteen more minutes."

"I'm not sure I can," she said and wiped her forehead with the back of her hand. She had to move more than he did.

"Go," he said. "I doubt I'll get a rush."

She shook her head. "We're a team," she said, and sat on the tiny red and green chair to the side of him, looking as if she would wilt before the shift was up.

He couldn't watch her or his own tiredness would overwhelm him. Instead he watched the stores closing: the Lord & Taylor's employees waiting impatiently by their cash registers; the Waldenbooks manager dragging her display shelf inside the store; the last stragglers in Musicland. The photographer had closed an hour before, and the beautician just after dinner. Only the jewelry store had its display lights on and the door to the street open.

The van was parked outside, near a streetlight, its single unbroken taillight turning the rain red. Exhaust fumes floated like fog over the pavement, and Matt frowned as he watched. The boy apparently hadn't bought his ring yet, or was coming back for another look.

A different teenage boy appeared from the driver's side. He grabbed the silver handle on the van's back and pulled the door open. The interior light didn't come on, but the streetlight provided just enough illumination to reveal several shotguns, handguns, and some ammunition.

"What are you looking at?" Matt's elf asked.

"Get mall security," he said, rising as he did so, "and dial 911."

Maybe he was making things up. Maybe. But his instincts told him that this was too odd to be coincidental. And his instincts had been on more than off these past fifteen years. Besides, he knew something about teenagers, shotguns, and determination. He put the red velvet rope with the *Santa Will Be Right Back* sign across the edge of the line, and walked to the jewelry store.

He didn't want to seem like he was coming to the rescue. That could make things messy. Instead, he played a new role: Santa as Christmas shopper. As he walked past the giant tree, he carefully bent over and whispered to the woman who was sitting on the fake park bench to get out of the way, something bad was going to happen, and to, as inconspicuously as she could, make sure no one else was in this vicinity.

She frowned at him as if he were crazy, then she looked over his shoulder. She must have seen the boys in the haze of the streetlight for she nodded once, stood, and walked toward a couple nuzzling near the packages.

The employee in the jewelry store, a slender woman whose hair was slipping out of its careful bun, was matching receipts to the cash register tape, an old-fashioned procedure not really necessary in these days of computers. Only a jewelry store would still continue that old-fashioned practice; it had high mark-up and low volume.

Outside, one of the boys slid his shotgun inside his open jacket. Matt made himself look away. He entered the jewelry store, whistling "Frosty the Snowman" and the clerk looked up, clearly startled. She opened her mouth, probably to tell him they were closing, when Matt smiled.

"Hello there!" Matt said in his jolliest voice. "I came to look at your engagement rings."

Without waiting for her response, he walked past the counter. "Get down," he whispered. "And look natural as you do it."

He didn't watch to see if she followed his instruction. Instead, he walked to the engagement ring display with its garish *Pay Nothing Until July!* sign.

The other boy closed the back of the van and joined his partner. They headed toward the store.

Matt reached up and hit the button that activated the mesh gate. It started down, too slowly for his comfort. The boys looked startled, then one of them grinned, pulled open the outside door, and slid under the gate.

The other boy followed.

On the mall side of the store, a second gate fell. Matt hadn't planned on that.

"Trying to be a hero, Pops?" the first boy asked as he pulled the shotgun out of his coat.

The clerk gasped, and Matt yelled, "Get down!" in case she hadn't hidden already. The gates made it all the way to the floor, clanging, trapping them inside.

The first boy held the shotgun on Matt. "You don't do nothing, Pops and everything'll be fine." He inclined his head toward his friend. "You," he said, smart enough not to use names, even though he didn't seem to care about hiding his acne scarred face. "Get the stuff."

The second boy had a sack, a red velvet one that look too similar to a Santa sack for comfort. He opened the display of diamond bracelets on the other side of the door, and began yanking them out.

Perhaps it was the bag. Perhaps it was the realization that these were boys, and inexperienced ones at that. Perhaps it was the knowledge that the clerk was safe, and whatever happened to Matt didn't matter. No one would care. No one would mourn. He was free to do as he wished, and what he wished was to stop this now.

Adrenaline pumped through him. He moved quicker than he thought he ever could.

He grabbed the engagement ring display case, and tossed it at the boy with the shotgun. The boy whirled, wasn't quick enough to shoot or get out of the way. The display hit him in the stomach and the gun fell out of his fingers, sliding on the red indoor-outdoor carpet.

Matt dove for the gun, and came up holding it, feeling absurdly like Rambo in a Santa costume. Time had slowed to a crawl—only once before had time done that to him—and it felt like each breath, each movement took a year.

The clerk screamed, and Matt shouted at the second boy to "Hold it!" The boy looked up and, startled, dropped the sack. He reached for the handgun he had stuck in his waistband.

"Touch it," Matt said, "and I will shoot you."

The boy held out his hands and slowly raised them, western-style. The other boy on the floor was struggling to get the display case off him, moaning as he did so, diamond rings scattered about him like shards of glass.

The sirens started first, coming closer and closer. Red and blue lights played across the cars outside, and Matt turned just enough to see mall security, watching through the mesh. The clerk, who still clutched her receipts, had her mouth open, her lower jaw trembling as if she had palsy.

"Let them in," Matt said.

It took a moment for his command to register, but when it did, she used a different control to open the gate on the mall side. The security cop came in, carrying the handcuffs he'd probably never used. He looked at Matt for instruction, and Matt nodded at the standing boy first.

"He's got a gun," Matt said, and the guard slipped a tentative hand around the boy's waist, grabbed the gun with two fingers, and, without taking his gaze off the boy's face, stepped backwards to set the gun on the counter.

For a moment Matt thought the boy would make a lunge for it, but he glanced at Matt and apparently didn't like what he saw there, so he didn't move. The first boy didn't seem to notice. The display had injured him somehow. He had stopped trying to move it, and had lain down in the position he had been in, still moaning quietly.

The red-and-blue lights filled the interior of the store, winking garishly off the diamonds, making Matt feel suddenly as if he were in a badly designed disco. The guard grabbed the boy and cuffed him, then the real cops came in the mall side, and took over, now that it was too late.

***

Two hours of story-telling in the manager's office, sitting in the only comfortable chair, looking at the out-of-date notices on the bulletin board flapping in the breeze coming out of a poorly placed heating duct. The cops who took his statement were sympathetic: they were the ones who had come on the scene, and they praised him for his quick thinking, his decision to trap the robbers, his whispered instructions to the elf, the customers, the clerk. But they said, because they had to, because it was true, sometimes things don't end so well. Sometimes the boy with the gun knows how to shoot, sometimes a well-pushed display case isn't very heavy at all, sometimes the other boy pays attention. You could have died, she could have died, and for what? Some franchise's diamond jewelry, which probably was insured anyway.

Matt nodded, listened, didn't defend himself, thinking not of the jewelry but of the weapons he'd seen in the van, the reports he'd been hearing too often lately about teenagers and guns, and the way they used them, not as tools, but as machines for slaughter. He hadn't been protecting jewelry; he'd been protecting the smiling baby who had grabbed his spirit-gummed beard and tried to chew it; the little girl who had laughed with her father with such complete joy. He had been protecting the small throne and the Ella Fitzgerald Christmas carols, and the gray light coming in from the atrium windows.

He had done it without thinking, and now that he could think, he knew he would do it all over again.

The cops must have seen the determination on his face, for they tried to reassure him. He had done well; he would be a hero; the boys were in custody. The robbery fit a pattern that had started a few weeks before, and even though the robberies were brazen, no one had been able to catch the thieves. They might stop now, after a taste of prison, a taste of pain, one of the cops said, and laughed. The display case had probably broken the kid's pelvis, and no man ever forgot that.

Matt waited until they were done, was cordial and kind until they dismissed him, and then went to the locker room to put on his street clothes. For the first time since he had quit five years before, he longed for a cigarette. The destructive impulse made him sadder than it should have, and he wondered what it was about the night that inspired him to make things worse.

**

THAT NIGHT HE WOKE in a cold sweat, the smooth polished feel of a shotgun still heavy in his hands, the heat of the summer's day covering him, the sound of a woman's voice, pleading, still echoing in his ears. He sat up in his rented bed and blinked in the unfamiliar darkness, the dream slowly fading.

It wasn't a dream really: it was a memory as clear as if it had happened just that night. The tinkle of the bell over the convenience store's glass door, the sharp smell of cheap perfume and plastic, the way the clerk had looked at him—terror making her face rounder, her eyes bigger, her mouth a silly but perfect circle. He lifted his grandfather's shotgun to his shoulder and shot out the cameras—all of them a perfect bulls-eye—and then he had tugged his ski mask to make sure it was in place.

The clerk had screamed after each shot, and when he finally turned the gun on her—his foster father's voice echoing in his head *Don't point a gun at anyone unless you mean to use it*—she had started pleading for her life: a single run-on sentence filled with spit and panic.

Don'tshootmemisterreallyI'lldoanythingyouwanthone stbutjustpleasedon'tshootmepleasepleasedon'tshootme.

For five days he had cased the place, realized it was a mom-and-pop organization that didn't like to do bank runs. It had a safe in the back filled with the day's takings, probably fifteen hundred dollars, maybe more, a lot of money in 1984. He had planned carefully, wearing someone else's clothes, bought at a Goodwill fifteen miles away, boots three sizes too big, with a heel that made him seem inches taller. A wig beneath his ski mask, and a Southern accent, spoken in a voice lower than his usual.

Because she had been so terrified, because he hadn't expected that, because he realized at the moment he stared down his gun at her that they both knew he could kill her, he took the money. Then he ripped out the phone, and made her lie down, telling her to wait until he had been gone fifteen minutes before she went for help. He set a wind-up toy on the floor and let it shuffle around so that she would still think he was in the store, then he slipped out the back door, the manager's door. He had a car waiting around the block—stolen that afternoon off a car lot in the same town as the Goodwill. He'd hot-wired the car, and left it running, figuring if someone else took it on a joyride it would be no big deal, might even get him off the hook.

But it was there, waiting for him, its exhaust rising like fog in the streetlights. He got in, removed his mask and wig, placed them in a plastic bag, put the money with them, and drove the car back to the lot. He replaced the $800—*Like New!* sign, and walked away as if he had never taken the car. His truck was parked behind a library a mile away. He walked awkwardly in the big boots. When he got to the truck, he slid into the cab, removed the boots, changed clothes, and threw them in the plastic bag. Then he removed the money, put it in an envelope, and stuck it in the glove box. He put a brick in the bag and tied it closed.

He drove all night, and the next day, just before dawn, as he was about to cross the Ohio River in Evansville, he took a side road, found a bridge no one was near, and chucked the plastic bag over the side. Then he drove back to the main highway and crossed into Kentucky, a new man. A man who had had nerve. A man who had stolen from someone else.

A man he could have killed if his finger had slipped.

He kept the money for two days, spreading it on the seat of his truck, never counting it, wearing gloves every time he touched it despite the August heat. And finally, he realized he'd never be able to spend it or add to it, that for the rest of his life, he'd see the clerk's round face, her big eyes and her silly circle of mouth, and know that for a few thousand dollars, he had nearly taken her life.

In Cairo, he put the money in an envelope, and mailed it back to the convenience store—its address burned in his brain from his five days of study, the 152 painted in black above the door like a neon sign every time he closed his eyes. He drove on to Memphis and told his first real lie to get his first honest job, and never looked back.

He had thought it would be easy money. But he hadn't realized he was still paying for it, even now.

He wrapped his arms around his knees, felt the thin rubbery blanket beneath the flesh of his forearms, the industrial smell of the sheets tickling his nose. No one was looking for him. The clerk would remember. He did. And maybe the mom-and-pop owners thought of that one time they'd been robbed. But no one else did. The cops who had worked the case were probably long gone.

He watched the true-life mystery shows and all the real-life cop dramas and never once had he seen the brief image of his own body, standing in that convenience store, pointing his grandfather's shotgun at the camera.

Still, because of tonight's heroics, he toyed with packing his bags, getting into the new truck, the one he'd had for the last year, and heading down I-5. It was still early. Maybe they were hiring Santas in Eugene, or Roseburg, or even in California.

But he couldn't do that. He finally understood what kind of peace he had shattered that night so long ago. He finally understood that he had done more than point a gun at a woman, and break a few laws. He had violated something else, someone's dream, perhaps, or a woman's illusion of safety.

He had been a punk kid, whose parents had died when he was twelve, and whom his various foster parents believed was responsible enough to need very little supervision. A punk kid with a shotgun and an attitude who figured he didn't need to work for anything, that he was smarter than all the rest—hadn't he graduated straight A's in high school without doing any work? He'd figured criminals who got caught were the ones who hadn't paid attention to the details, and he was determined to make it rich by thinking.

Only he hadn't. He hadn't done any thinking at all.

Perhaps that burst of anger in the jewelry store hadn't been aimed at two teenage boys violating a mall with guns and a Santa bag. Maybe the anger had been at a single teenage boy who thought he could have the easy life by staking out a place, picking up a shotgun, and taking money from people who had spent long dirty hours earning it.

Maybe, just maybe, he had come a lot farther than he thought.

***

THE NEXT MORNING, he dressed early and stared at his bags, refusing to let himself pack them. He went to the mall on time, saw, as he got off the bus, the vans decorated with the logos of all the local news channels. Inside, a crowd of cameras studied Santa's Village, but didn't film the grandfather. Instead, they were waiting for Matt.

He hesitated. They didn't recognize him in his street clothes. He could turn around and leave, and no one would be the wiser. Then, of course, someone would investigate his résumé, realize that there was no Professor Sturtz at Gustavus Adolphus, and the entire story would turn bizarre in the space of an afternoon.

The jewelry store was open, the sole employee with the official rumpled look of a manager facing more stress than he expected. The damaged display had been placed behind the counter, but a cameraman was asking, rather loudly, that the display be moved back to its original location.

Matt bit his lower lip, then felt a hand on his arm. The mall manager smiled uncertainly at him, and said, "They want you in the Santa suit, if that's all right."

Matt nodded, then felt some of the tension leave his shoulders. Not that he was worried about being caught—whatever happened, happened—but because he was worried about ruining this moment for everyone else. Every now and then a mere mortal, dressed as Santa, did something spectacular. It helped the kids believe. It brought a smile to the face of weary parents. It gave the season a shining layer of gold.

He changed into his suit, made an appearance, and let the cameras turn their shiny lenses on him, while the reporters asked questions, posed him in the scene of the crime, in the village, with a volunteer child. He smiled and laughed and waited patiently until it was all done, and when they finally left to find another human interest tale or to chase an ambulance, he winked at his elf—a different woman from the night before—and asked if she was ready to get back to business. She was.

The children filed through, the photos were snapped, gifts were given. He held each wriggling little body as if it were more precious than diamonds, and he made sure each little wish was passed on, just as he had before.

It had been this that had changed him, this small tradition, seeing how important it was to each child, each parent, waiting patiently in his line. It wasn't the deed that mattered so much as the life lived. His had been empty, purposely, except for this one tradition, this single month where he was at his best. Somehow that pushed him farther, made him do more than he ever thought he could.

He would still wander away from Portland, and Matt Sturtz would disappear forever. But there was an old name, nearly forgotten, a real name that could be dusted off, along with dreams and goals, and perhaps the person who owned that name could find a way of contributing more than a merry laugh, a few empty promises, and a jolly red suit.

He had a few weeks to think about how he would do that, what would be his best plan. And no matter what he actually did—whether he went back to that tiny Midwestern town and confessed or whether he found another way to pay for his sins—he knew, that when he gave the suit back, he wouldn't wait until next Thanksgiving to become the person he wanted to be. He wouldn't let the season fade. He would work at keeping the shine, every day of the coming year.

Snow Angels

S O Gramps took them down to the road anyway. Bobberts stuck his hands in his pockets. His fingers found his dad's Swiss Army knife. He didn't even get to use it. Dad was kinda mean about that.

You don't use knives to cut trees, Bobs, Dad said. *That's what the chainsaw is for.*

But Bobberts brought the knife so they wouldn't need the chainsaw. Last year, Daddy said the chainsaw was why Gramps took Bobberts and Sarah to the car before the Christmas tree was cut.

Too much could go wrong with chainsaws.

So him and Sarah got sent to the car again. This time, Bobberts was mad.

Sarah didn't care. She just skipped ahead, happy to be in the trees and the snow. She liked outside, she liked playing, she liked it all.

She didn't know there was cool stuff they couldn't do.

Dad said Bobberts would get to do it "some day."

Bobberts was beginning to think "some day" meant "never."

The snow on the path was muddy. You could see the rocks underneath it. Bobberts kicked one, and Gramps laughed.

"It's not that much fun, kiddo," Gramps said. "They get a chainsaw and just slice through the tree. It's over in five seconds."

Bobberts nodded. Dad said the same thing, but that didn't mean it was true. Bobbert'd never seen somebody use a chainsaw—Dad said he was too little. He was nine now, and tall for his age. Everybody said so.

He wasn't little any more.

Sarah skipped through the trees. "There's the car," she said, pointing.

Their car and two others. Those weirdo people who were walking with Daddy and the tree guy into the woods. Bobberts didn't want to call it a farm, because he didn't see pigs and cows and horses. It was just a woods with lots of Christmas trees.

Gramps reached the car first, and unlocked it. Then he rubbed his hands together. "You kids get inside," he said. "I gotta see a man about a dog."

As he walked back up the path, Sarah looked at Bobbert. "There's dogs?" she asked.

Bobberts shook his head. "Gramps says that when he's gotta go Number One."

Sarah giggled and put her hands over her mouth. She was still little. Four. Mom said everybody had to watch out for her. Small and pretty and all girl, that's what Mom said. But Mom never saw the goofy side of Sarah, except that one time. That time she was really, really little and trying to learn Bobberts' name. She couldn't say Bobbie, so Daddy tried to teach her Robert.

It came out Bobberts, and it stuck.

Sometimes Bobberts liked it. Sometimes he wished she wasn't so cute so everybody remembered everything she said.

She took his hand and tugged. "Lookie the snow."

She pointed at the field above the cars. The trees didn't start right away. There was one big pile of white.

He knew what she was thinking. Sarah'd been like this ever since the snow started. One big pile of white and she wanted to dive in it.

Finally Daddy taught her snow angels just so she wouldn't go running into the big pile of white and dive into a rock or something.

"Don't wanna," Bobberts said. He'd get colder than he already was. Besides, big kids didn't make snow angels.

"C'mon." Sarah tugged him toward the empty whiteness. Bobberts looked around for Gramps, but didn't see him. The trees were pretty thin right near the road.

Gramps taught Bobberts how to pee in the woods last year.

First rule, Gramps had said, *go deep enough that nobody can see you.*

A car went by on the road, kicking up slush. Bobberts winced. He was gonna get wet and cold no matter where he was.

"You do it," he said.

Sarah stuck her tongue out at him, and ran up the hill. She stopped smack in the middle, turned to face the road, spread her arms, and fell backwards.

Snow puffed up around her.

Bobberts kicked the snow off a nearby rock and perched on it. He could see Sarah and he could see the path. Far away, he heard the moan of a chainsaw, and closer, the slam of a car door.

Sarah made a perfect angel. Then she sat up, and wiped the snow off her face. "*C'mon*," she said.

Bobberts shook his head.

She put her thumb to her nose and waggled her fingers at him. Then she got up, moved a few steps down, and flopped again.

How many snow angels was she gonna make?

Mom would be so mad at him. Sarah wasn't wearing her mittens, and her coat was gonna get soaked.

Bobberts looked up the trail for Gramps, but still didn't see him. Then something caught his eye. A guy was standing in the thin trees, staring down at Sarah. The guy was wearing gray, just like the trees, and he blended into the hillside.

Bobberts felt a little shiver. How long had that guy been there?

Adults were so creepy.

Sarah sat up again, took off her hat, and shook snow from it. Then she stuck it on her blonde curls. This time she didn't look at Bobberts at all.

This time, she went farther down the hill.

He saw the pattern she was making. Snow angels, like those cutouts you make with folded papers and scissors. She was really good at stuff like that. Mom said Sarah was gonna be an artist one day.

Bobberts sighed. This was taking forever. Daddy said only five minutes and it had to be lots more than that. The chainsaw still rumbled back there.

The tree wasn't even that great. There was a bigger, fuller one right next to it, but Daddy said it wouldn't fit in the front door. Gramps'd winked at Bobberts and said Daddy just didn't want to carry it all the way back to the car.

Bobberts rubbed his nose with the back of his hand. He was getting snow snot. Nose drips that happened out in the cold, that's what snow snot was. Gramps said so. Sarah said it was just icky, and Bobberts agreed.

Sarah.

He looked up. She was in the middle of her fourth angel. She'd done 'em so perfect that they looked like they were hanging along the slope. She'd fallen on her own footprints, so you couldn't see them at all.

Then that guy came out of the trees. He snuck out, like he didn't want nobody to see him. He walked right into the middle of the fourth angel, screwing it all up, and bent down.

Sarah screamed.

Bobberts stood up. No Gramps. Nobody, just that chainsaw still whirring far away.

The man grabbed Sarah by her arms and pulled her up. She was screaming and kicking and biting just like Mom taught them to do.

The man didn't care. He just grabbed her like Daddy did sometimes, and tucked her under his arm. She was yelling, "Bobberts! Bobberts!"

And Bobberts didn't know what to do.

The man was going back toward the trees.

Bobberts looked at the path, but it was empty. He bit his lower lip, and headed up the hillside.

When someone gets you, Mom always said, *you do what you gotta do to get away.*

She never said what you gotta to do when someone got Sarah.

Bobberts was breathing hard. He had to hurry. That guy had Sarah and she was screaming and he was scared—what if that guy was one of those guys who hurt little kids? What if they never see Sarah again?

Bobberts could hear himself breathe. It sounded louder than the screaming, louder than that weird saw noise. Louder than the guy yelling at Sarah to shut up.

But the guy had his back to Bobberts, and he was hurrying.

Through the trees, Bobberts could see the car. It was the same one that had passed earlier, the one that sent slush everywhere.

The guy'd seen Sarah and come back for her.

That made Bobberts even madder.

They were almost at the trees. Bobberts had to do something.

He ran the last few steps, slipping on the snow. And that's when he thought of it: He was wearing really good boots (Mom made him) but that guy was wearing Nikes.

Nikes weren't made for snow.

Bobberts reached the guy and grabbed the guy's back leg. The guy's front foot slipped. The guy turned and yanked at the same time, sliding on the snow. Bobberts let go.

The guy fell on his belly, and went down the hill like he was on a sled, dropping Sarah. She was crying really hard now. The fall had hurt her too.

Bobberts half ran, half slid down near them.

"Sarah!" Bobberts yelled. "Run away!"

Sarah was stretched out in the snow. She was still crying. Sometimes she could cry so hard she'd forget what she was doing.

Bobberts pointed to the path. "Get Gramps!"

She stumbled. The guy crawled toward her, getting close to Bobberts.

And that's when Bobberts kicked him.

The guy rolled onto his back. He was really big and really mean-looking. Bobberts was never so scared in his whole life, not even when the sixth grade boys ganged up on him.

"Boy or girl," the man said in an icky voice. "Don't matter to me."

He pulled Bobberts to him, but didn't knock Bobberts down.

The guy grinned at him, and a shiver went through Bobberts. A shiver, and an ick, and a fear like he'd never had.

So he kicked again. Kicked and kicked in the place Gramps said no boy ever really liked, and the man was squealing and rolling away and holding himself, and Sarah was gone—where'd she go?—and there wasn't sound, except Bobberts' breathing and the guy squealing and the bam of Bobberts' boot hitting the guy.

Then the guy's hand grabbed Bobberts' foot, and Bobberts went down, just like Sarah did when she was making snow angels. Only he was surprised and the air went right out of his body.

"Don't make no difference." The man's voice sounded airy now, and kinda weird. He sat up. His skin was sickly looking, like he was gonna puke.

The guy was bigger than the sixth-grade boys and Bobberts couldn't stop them from beating him up. This guy would win. This guy would hurt him.

But Momma said when someone gets you, you do what you gotta do to get away.

Bobberts slipped his hand in his pocket. Daddy was already mad at him about the knife. He told Bobberts that Bobberts was too young to use it.

Do what you can, Momma whispered in his ear.

Bobberts dug the knife out, and snicked it open and jabbed it in the guy's arm. The guy screamed and reached for the knife, but Bobberts remembered to pull it out so that Daddy wouldn't get mad that it got stolen, and the guy was calling Bobberts bad names, and pulling even harder on Bobberts' boot, and Bobberts stabbed the guy's arm again, and again, and then Bobberts missed, and the knife slipped and hit the guy in the leg.

The guy really screamed, and far away, Bobberts heard Gramps yelling his name, then yelling for Daddy, and then just yelling.

But the guy was screaming and rolling away from Bobberts and blood was squirting like the guy's leg was one giant water pistol, and snow was getting all red.

The guy'd let go of Bobberts' ankle, but it took him a minute to tell because his ankle still hurt. His whole body hurt from falling and running out of air, and the guy was still screaming, and Daddy was yelling now, and Bobberts got up and tripped his way over Sarah's snow angels to the path.

Gramps took his arm, and Daddy was running down from the woods, and Sarah was crying, and the tree guy was yelling into his phone about police and help and the weirdo couple behind him wanted to use the chainsaw to scare the guy, and Gramps said it wouldn't be necessary because he'd be dead soon anyway.

And at first Bobberts thought Gramps meant the guy would be dead because Gramps would see to it, but Gramps didn't mean that at all. The guy had stopped screaming and the blood wasn't squirting any more, and the snow was so red it didn't look like snow, and the blood was dripping down the footprints into Sarah's snow angels, decorating them like Momma decorated her Christmas cookies, with a touch of red over the white.

Then Daddy reached them and grabbed Sarah and looked at Bobberts and Gramps said, "The kid saved them both," and Daddy looked like he was gonna cry, and Bobberts knew exactly why.

He held out the knife. It was bent funny and covered with gunk. He said, "I'm sorry, Daddy. I think I broke it."

And Daddy took the knife from him, dropped it onto the path, and pulled Bobberts to his other side.

Bobberts clung onto Daddy's jeans, feeling Daddy's leg shake, or maybe Bobberts was shaking, and Sarah was crying, and Gramps was telling everybody to stay on the path, and Daddy said, "It's okay," but they all knew it really wasn't.

The tree guy couldn't wait and he had to go see if the mean guy was all right, and Gramps kept shaking his head. Bobberts wanted to get out of there, but he knew they couldn't go yet.

"Daddy," Bobberts said. "You forgot the tree."

And Daddy laughed, only it didn't sound like a Daddy-laugh. It sounded kinda shaky and weird, and he looked at Gramps, and he said, "I think we're gonna get a tree from the store," and Bobberts didn't know what that meant, but he nodded anyway.

Sarah wiped her face off, and lifted her head, and said, "I was just making angels, Daddy."

"I know," Daddy said. "I know. And they protected you, honey."

"Uh-uh," Sarah said. "That was Bobberts."

And Bobberts smiled, even though he was shaking. He smiled and reached for his sister, and hugged her, even though it was a baby thing to do.

And nobody said nothing, nobody except Gramps, who said, "We got hot cocoa in the car," like it was a reward.

And maybe it was.

Like smiling against his dad's leg, and hugging his sister, and being really, really glad that nobody said nothing about the knife, lying bloody and broken in the snow.

Doubting Thomas

*T*OMMY ULRICK DISCOVERED THE SCAM when he was six. He remembered everything about the night clearly: the winter dampness in the air, the smell of wood smoke mixed with ocean, waking on his flannel sheets with an urgency that seemed only to happen in childhood. He slipped out of bed and hurried to the bathroom—one of those herky-jerky emergencies where he jiggled all the way, holding himself, and praying he'd arrive on time.

Which he did, just barely. He remembered the relief, and as the relief grew, so did his chill. Someone had left the large bathroom window open, letting the December cold inside, allowing people on the street below to see his most private moment.

He glanced out—still too compromised to pull the window closed—to see if anyone was watching. The neighborhood Christmas lights were off, the houselights were off, even the few porch lights that stayed on late were off. Only the streetlight broke the darkness, casting pools of pale light through the thin fog.

He was safe. No one could see him. He shook himself off, tucked himself back inside his flannel pajamas, reached to close the window— and froze.

There was movement on the roof of the house across the street.

Well, not a house, actually. It was too big to be a house. It was the Sutter place, which his mother used to call, "the only bona fide mansion on the Central Oregon Coast." Later when he learned the history of it, when he was older and into such things, he discovered that his mother had been wrong –there had been other mansions, just none as visible, none quite as centrally located as the one on the street below their little two-bedroom ranch.

Still he struggled, trying to get the window closed, the wind blowing against him, plastering the ice-cold snap buttons against his bare chest. Somehow the battle became him against the window, and he was losing.

Then he saw the movement again. And what had looked like shadows became three men dressed as Santa Claus, dark sacks against their backs, struggling with the dormer on the side of the house.

He watched, horrified, as they tugged it open. Then they disappeared inside, one by one, none of them looking up at him, none of them noticing.

Then, from inside, white-gloved hands pulled the dormer closed.

***

Oh, Tommy did all the right things. He woke his parents, who called the police. His dad stared out the bathroom window a long time, as if he could see something different. Tommy stared too, pointed out the sleigh on the front lawn, saying it hadn't been there when he saw the men, but his dad just ignored him.

So did the police after they arrived. They walked around the Sutter place, saw no evidence of false entry, saw nothing out of the ordinary, and said so. They came up to Tommy's house, listened to his story, and told his parents not to let him watch so much television.

Then they left.

Tommy's mom made him use the bathroom one more time before he went to bed. No one had closed the window and as he looked out on the mansion below, he saw that the sleigh was gone.

Only this time, he didn't tell anyone. He snuck back to bed, pulled the covers to his chin, and shivered for the rest of the night.

***

Christmas was never the same after that. Tommy made sure there were no Santa Claus decorations in the house. He wouldn't sit on the Santa man's lap at the mall, and he wouldn't watch any Santa shows on television. He told his parents that he didn't believe, and they seemed saddened by it, but they thought it understandable.

After all, the Sutter place had been robbed that night. Apparently the police had arrived too late to do anything about it. Tommy had seen something. Turned out the dormer window was askew. There was even a bit of extra ash in the fireplace that next morning, and men's shoe prints tracking all over the house.

One of the police officers came by to apologize and to take Tommy's statement again. The theory was that the men had used the Santa Claus outfits as a ruse to get into the house, figuring they could pose on the roof like Christmas decorations if a car went by.

Brilliant, the police called it.

Humbug, Tommy would have said to himself if he had known the word then. Complete and total humbug.

He had seen the dark side of Santa, and was never ever going to be the same again.

***

CHILDHOOD LOST, CYNICISM FOUND. Outwardly Tommy Ulrick was the same as all the other little boys of his age, unless someone mentioned Santa Claus. It got so bad that his parents used to warn people not to use the name. At Christmas, he became sullen and fearful, and there didn't seem to be anything anyone could do about it.

His parents thought he would grow out of it. It was a phase, they said, brought on by a traumatic childhood event, and, as Tommy got older and realized that his attitude toward the Jolly Old Elf was socially unacceptable, he stopped talking about it.

Instead, he turned inward. He studied. He learned everything he could about the enemy, and what he saw he didn't like.

It was, he came to understand, the biggest fraud ever perpetrated on the public. A round-cheeked old man masquerading as a saint who gave toys to children, all the while using those children to hide his own greed. In fact, the old man used his scam to teach greed.

In Tommy—now Thomas—Ulrick's life, Christmas ceased to be about love and peace and goodwill toward all men. Instead, it turned into a holiday about stuff. Who bought the most, who spent the most, who got the most. Even people who belonged to other religions gave into the Christmas frenzy. They treated it as a secular holiday, so their kids wouldn't be left out of the stuff-getting.

It was, Thomas realized, a shameful thing.

And when he turned thirty, he'd finally had enough.

***

LATER, HE FIGURED, everything culminated that year. His parents had died in a car accident the year before. He'd taken a leave of absence from his big city reporter's position—a forced leave of absence: reporters are supposed to do everything they can to get a story, but apparently "everything" did *not* include breaking a few minor privacy laws. His third fiancée left him just like all the others had when she realized that he hated Christmas. Apparently his fiancées could tolerate different religions, different attitudes toward money, but not a bah-humbugish attitude toward Christmas.

It was, he discovered, the ultimate deal-breaker.

So on Christmas Eve of that year, he sat down at his kitchen table, in his comfortable two-bedroom ranch style house in the Portland suburb of Beaverton, and, like he used to do when he was starting an article, made a list.

1. Adults all acknowledge there is no Santa Claus.

2. Children are encouraged to believe in Santa Claus.

3. Santa doesn't give gifts. Parents do, thus perpetuating the myth.

4. From Halloween on, people see Santa Claus on the streets, and think nothing of it.

5. People decorate their homes with Santa Claus iconography, making it easy for fake Santas to hide.

6. The only thing that people do when they see a Santa is give him something. (Does the Salvation Army really still exist? Do they sanction those little red change boxes? Is this a direct part of the scam or is this something else encouraged by the Evil Santa Brigade?)

7. Was the lump of coal more than a metaphor? Perhaps, in the early years, the Santa thieves left only a lump of coal when they cleaned out a house.

8. Naughty or nice. Who's to determine? Based on what criteria?

9. Robberies increase supposedly because houses are more vulnerable. People in the holiday spirit aren't as vigilant.

10. Fires increase. Arson to cover up robberies?

11. More people commit suicide during the holidays than at any other time of the year. Real suicides? Or more cover-ups—killed when they discover someone who isn't supposed to be in the house?

12. Was Clement Moore in on this?

13. How long has this been going on?

Thomas stopped, chilled to the bone. One man against a centuries-old tradition of duplicity and thievery.

He had to stop this. But how?

***

IT CAME TO HIM as he woke up the next morning. There had to be a grain of truth to everything in the myth.

He sat up, his frayed cotton sheets pooled around his waist. He was willing to believe that the original Santa thieves went down chimneys, just like the stories. A roof was a great access point for a robber, and a hundred years ago, children used to climb into chimneys to clean them. Skinny children, but children nonetheless. He didn't believe that fat old men slid down chimneys—but that was the impossibility that made the idea seem so ludicrous. Better to go back to the truth.

And he would wager that a lot of Santa's Helpers went through the front doors too.

He rubbed his hands together. He felt like he was finally onto something.

He got out of bed, and grabbed his robe, sliding it on as he made his way to the kitchen. He didn't believe that Santa operated from the North Pole—too cold, too remote, too impractical—but he would wager that there was a hideout. It didn't have to be very big—not like the factory portrayed in all those stupid Christmas movies. After all, Santa wasn't making toys. He was stealing stuff.

The hideout had to be a place to run to, a place to hide, a place to split up the wealth, like the Hole-in-the-Wall of Western Outlaw lore.

And if he found the Hole in the Wall, the hideout, he found the bad guys.

He had the power to stop this scam once and for all.

***

IT WAS EASIER THAN HE THOUGHT. It just took time.

After all, he had data from thirty years of collecting. His newspaper training made him an excellent sleuth. He searched for robberies, fires, and suicides, throwing in a few surprise deaths from heart failure and a couple of thwarted attempts.

He made a cybermap and marked out all the hits in the United States for the last fifty years, searching for a pattern—and what he found terrified him. If his assumptions were true, and he had no reason to think they weren't—then he was dealing with something so large that he could barely contemplate it.

Every state got hit, every county, every town—and in the right statistical proportions. In fact, that's what gave the plot away. The statistics were too perfect. No cluster of suicides in Denver in any one year, for example, or no extra fires in San Jose. Apparently the statisticians hadn't noticed that every city had just about the same number of robberies, deaths, and fires in the weeks before Christmas. The ever-so-slight variations came from what he would consider to be unconnected events—gang killings, insurance fraud arson, and the robberies caused by non-affiliated thieves (whom, he noted, usually got caught).

He expanded his search to include Britain and Western Europe, and found fewer incidences there, although those too were statistically perfect. Going back a hundred years, he found higher incidences in England; he figured that was probably where the scam originated.

Thomas spent weeks analyzing the information and figured that the hideout was in the United States where the pickings were good. There were probably several sub-hideouts, but the main one—if he were the guy planning all of this—had to be centrally located.

Unless…

He paused, hands over the keys, as inspiration struck again.

All those greeting cards, posters, t-shirts. *Images* everywhere of Santa in a swimsuit and loud floral-print shirt, lounging in a beach chair on the sand, chubby ankles crossed while he stared at a pristine ocean. Those pictures never depicted Santa on a Hawaiian beach or relaxing on California's sultry sands.

Santa was always in Florida, generally Miami Beach, and he was always grinning at the camera.

Taunting someone—taunting Thomas—to find him.

Thomas scanned the Florida information. The farther south he went, the more evidence he found—in the lack of evidence, of course. Fewer Christmas fires (statistically attributable to the warm weather, the lack of heaters, the fact that Christmas trees didn't dry out as quickly), fewer suicides (statistically attributable the advanced age of the population; if they lived that long, they wouldn't throw what was left away), and surprisingly, given the wealth of the area, fewer robberies (statistically attributable to the fact that most people traveled *to* Florida during the holidays; fewer vacant homes). Heart attacks were up, but they didn't fall into his mathematical model because very few of those were a surprise, again given the advance age of the population.

He went to his hardcopy cabinet and pulled one of his many Santa souvenirs out of the postcard file. Santa, wearing sunglasses five times too big, a red-and-orange checked shirt a size too small, and matching orange shorts which revealed pale hairy legs, waved out of the image. *Wish You Were Here,* said the red lettering across the top.

"I will be," he promised the Jolly Old Elf. "Soon."

***

FOR SOME REASON, the thievery began again in Gainesville. Orlando was safe—maybe because Santa liked it there, or spread out his Florida vacation spots–but anything north of Gainesville was as fair as the rest of the western world.

He spent the months before Christmas studying the maps, searching for patterns. He finally found them. Simple, elegant, and difficult to see. The thieves worked in an alphabetical or numerical pattern by street name. Each state was assigned a letter or number, and then the pattern shifted clockwise from year to year. In other words, if Main was the "A" street in the first year, the next year it would be the "Z" street. The pattern worked the same with numbers.

Once the state's number or letter had been assigned, the thieves picked the exact street according to housing prices and the quality of the neighborhood. Then they probably staked a few houses out. It sounded like a lot of work, but it wasn't.

If he was right, that year Florida was the "D" street and the "30th" state. Gainesville was a number town— there were a lot of thirties. Southwest thirties, thirties with streets, thirties with avenues. Thomas scanned all the possible thirties and came up with what he considered to be a jackpot—30ᵗʰ Terrace, an area where the homes were worth half a million or more with lots of acreage, right in the middle of the city. Right smack in the center of that region was a house that had been owned for a couple of decades by the same people, philanthropists by their profile, who didn't believe in home security systems.

He did a bit more research, discovered that the home's owners boarded their dog and canceled their newspaper delivery every year just before Christmas. He didn't even break a sweat to find out that information. He imagined the Santa Stealers had all of this down to a science.

On December 18, he had lunch with fiancée number three—for old times sake, he said—and told her he was going out of town. He gave her a key to his safe deposit box, and told her to open it if he wasn't back by the first of the year.

She looked at him as if he were crazy, which was how she had been looking at him for the last year or more. But she agreed, which was all that mattered.

Then he flew to Orlando, rented a black sports car, and drove to Gainesville.

***

HE HADN'T DONE A REAL honest-to-god stakeout in nearly five years. Back when he was young and hungry, he got a lot of his information just spying on people. The older he got, the more he used legal information obtained through records, and then as he learned his way around computers, he found more and more fascinating things illegally.

But this was no longer a computer sort of case. This required diligence, wakefulness, and quick-thinking.

He slept during the day at a cheap hotel on the highway and watched the empty house at night. No neighbors nearby to report him, no big dogs to bark. By December 22nd, he was beginning to think the house was too perfect, or his research suspect. He hadn't seen hide nor hair of a sleigh or eight tiny reindeer or anything else near the target house.

But he knew that these Santa Bandits struck all the way through December 25th. He just had to be patient.

And finally, at 4 a.m. on the morning of December 24th, his patience paid off. He was keeping himself awake by making condensation rings on the driver's side window, when he heard a car engine, a sound he hadn't heard after midnight in this neighborhood since he started his vigil.

He slumped down in the sports car's bucket seat, and watched as a dark colored late model minivan with its lights off pulled into the house's long gravel driveway. When he was sure the occupants could no longer see his car, he grabbed his binoculars and climbed over the shifting column to the passenger seat. There he leaned against the dash and watched.

A chill ran up his spine, and for a moment, he touched his six-year-old self.

Instead he focused on the movement he saw on the empty house's roof. Three men, just like he had seen twenty-four years before, dressed as Santa, carrying black bags over their shoulders—empty bags. The men balanced precariously on the steep roof, climbing to its peak. Then the first man reached over and pulled open a window that probably led to an attic. He slid in, head first, as if he were diving into a pool.

The other two followed.

And Thomas, his six-year-old self still closer to the surface than he wanted the boy to be, slipped out of the car to pee.

***

LESS THAN AN HOUR LATER, the men emerged the way they entered, full bags over their shoulders. They slid down the back roof, presumably to the van, which he hadn't been able to see.

Then, lights out, it left the driveway.

Thomas waited until it was nearly a block away before he started the rental. He followed, his lights out too, keeping a discreet distance.

The van's lights came on at the end of 30th Terrace, and from then on all driving was normal. Thomas tailed them, mentally congratulating himself for a) practicing that skill a lot before and b) renting a sports car. He was able to keep up.

As he drove, he called 911 and reported the break-in. Step one of his plan.

Just as he expected, when they hit the highway, they headed south. But they didn't go to Miami, like he expected.

Instead, they went to Orlando, where the waiters sang, men dressed like giant mice, and make-believe was part of the air.

His enemy was craftier than even Thomas thought. He should have known that Miami Beach was a ruse. It was the Florida part with the grain of truth to it.

When they finally stopped, he felt a surge of disappointment. He couldn't help himself. He had been hoping for something interesting, something unique.

Instead, they pulled into a strip mall in one of the outlying areas of Orlando, where the rents were cheaper and the businesses cheesier. They drove around back and he followed, but he knew where they were going. He didn't have to be a rocket scientist to figure that one out.

The biggest store on the strip. It had a candy-cane striped door, giant toy soldiers guarding either side. Decorated Christmas trees stood in front of each window, and a couple of plaster elves looked like they had just finished painting the store's name on its sign: *The Christmas Cottage*.

But that wasn't the biggest giveaway. The biggest giveaway were the Santa statues—all three of them. On the roof.

***

THOMAS HAD HIS VIDEO CAMERA, his microcassette tape recorder, and a digital camera with a telephoto lens. As he got out of the car, he called 911, said he saw some suspicious activity at the Christmas Cottage, and that he was getting out of his car to investigate.

The dispatch urged him not to, of course, but he hung up, as if he were a zealous citizen. Which, he supposed, he was.

He left the digital zoom in the car, clicked on the microcassette recorder, and headed toward the back. The sun was just starting to come up, sending pale yellow light across the flat Florida landscape.

As he expected, the van was parked directly behind the Christmas Cottage. The store's back doors were open, and no one was in sight.

He slipped inside. The back of the store was bigger than he thought, almost a store in and of itself. There was an assortment of boxes, all of them clearly merchandise, some open with ornaments or tinsel hanging out. But an open storage door on the left side revealed items that didn't belong in a Christmas store.

He moved toward it as quietly as he could. Voices were coming from the storefront, talking amiably, as if someone were telling a story. Probably relating the events of the night.

When he got closer to the storage door, he stopped and made sure he was in shadow. He needed a place to hide if the thieves came back. He found the perfect spot behind a man-sized box, and set to work.

With shaking hands he raised the video camera to his right eye. Mentally, he cataloged as he went: coin collections, artwork, and jewelry—so much jewelry that his entire body felt numb. Then there were silver—from flatware to pitchers, the antiques (all small enough to carry), and the occasional high-end television.

He was nearly done with a white-gloved hand grabbed his wrist, pulling the camcorder down.

"Ho, ho, ho," a deep voice said with more cheer than seemed appropriate to the situation.

Another hand took the camcorder away. Thomas started to protest, but stopped. He was busted. He had to think clearly now.

He turned slowly, and tried not to let his surprise show.

The man standing behind him was no more than five feet tall, with white hair down to his shoulders and a fluffy white beard. He was wearing a red suit with real fur, and shiny black boots. He ho-hoed again and his stomach jiggled, just like that infamous bowl full of jelly. He had an unlit pipe in his bow-shaped mouth, and his blue eyes did twinkle merrily—at Thomas's expense.

All of the images of Santa were on the mark—if one ignored the height problem.

"Little Tommy Ulrick," the man said. "I wondered if you would be a problem."

"H-How do you know who I am?" Thomas asked.

The man tsk-tsked. "Tommy, of all people, you have to ask? I'm Santa. I know everything."

"Yeah," Thomas said, blessing his own forethought in having the microcassette recorder running. "That's why you have to steal for a living."

Claus—or whoever he was—sighed. "Ah, an explanation man. Somehow I would have thought you had it all worked out, Tommy."

"Thomas. And all I want to know is why."

"Not how? Not all the particulars?"

"No," Thomas said. He finally had control of his voice again. "Only why."

Claus's twinkling eyes narrowed. "I wouldn't have figured you for a true believer."

"I'm not," Thomas said. "I'm a reporter. I have a Need to Know."

Claus made a rude sound. "A need to spy, you mean. Which I would have thought that incident when you were six cured you of."

"Naw," Thomas said. "Just made me even more curious. So. Why do you do it?"

Claus sighed. "I hate this part."

His friends came through the doorway. They were even shorter. Even though they were wearing jeans and ratty Marlins t-shirts, they looked like Santa's elves. Which they probably were.

"Another one, Boss?"

"Whatcha gonna do this time?"

Claus ignored them. Instead he stared at Thomas.

"Look, I'll split the loot with you fifty-fifty if you just don't ask for the explanation."

"Too late," Thomas said. "I already did."

One of the elves laughed. "Gotta tell him, Boss. Don't you just hate those magic rules?"

"How much time do we have?" the other elf asked.

"If he called 911, maybe ten more minutes."

"Plenty of time, Boss."

"Someone trained you, right?" Thomas asked. "This is like a worldwide scam that's been going on for centuries. The original Santa was, what? a real Fagan? A man who trained his cohorts from childhood?"

"I am the original Santa," Claus said.

This time it was Thomas's turn to make the rude noise.

"I *am*," Claus said. He turned to the elves. "I really do hate this part."

"Get it over with, Boss," the first elf said, then crossed his arms and leaned against the wall. "I'm keeping an ear out for the coppers."

"Pigs," the other elf corrected.

Thomas frowned at them. Coppers? Pigs? Was their slang really out of date? Or were they faking it just for him?

"You figured it out," Claus said. "You know that part of the myth is true, and part of it is convenient. Well, I'm just a jolly old elf. Really."

"More like a leprechaun," the elf said.

"Or even that Coyote character," the other elf said.

"A trickster?" Thomas asked. That part he hadn't figured out.

Claus put one finger beside his nose and pointed at Thomas with the other hand. Thomas ducked, as if he expected something magical to happen to him.

Claus chuckled, a deep rolling laugh that seemed to fill the room. "You *do* believe."

"I know something was up," Thomas said. "I figured out your theft pattern. I know about your units. I even figured you were in Florida."

"But you don't know why, and it bothers you." Claus let his fingers drop.

"Yes," Thomas said, if he could keep the trio talking, they'd stay here until the cops arrived. Then he'd have everything on tape. "If you have magic, why steal?"

"Magic requires belief. A few people still believe, but for the most part, rationalists have taken over. About the time Claus started, don't you know."

Thomas did know. He just hadn't put it together.

"So," Claus said, "if I can get people to believe in a jolly old elf for part of a year, why then, I have a bit of my powers. Not all, any more. Just enough."

"But why use them to steal?"

Claus frowned. "An immortal has-been needs a way to maintain his lifestyle."

"At the expense of people's homes? At the expense of their lives?"

"Oh, crap, Boss," one of the elves said. "This is a live one."

Claus continued to ignore them. "Mistakes happen," he said. "The deaths are always regrettable."

"Regrettable?" Thomas's voice rose. Then he cleared his throat, too late, of course. They'd probably already heard the panic.

"I think I hear sirens, Boss," one of the elves said.

"Me too." The second elf's ears—which really were pointed—started to twitch.

"You go," Claus said. "I'll handle this guy."

"Boss, we're going to need a new hideout," the first elf said.

"We'll worry about that later. Just go."

They scurried out the back and closed the double doors. After a moment, Thomas heard the van start.

Claus was smiling at him. It wasn't a nice smile. "I have so many options. I could let those cops you called find you here with the loot. I could kill you. Or I could make use of you."

"You'd make me a part of your thieving band?"

"Don't be silly," Claus said. "You wouldn't last a year. I can see through to Naughty and Nice, and you got waaaay too much Nice in you. That's probably why you searched me out, even though you say it's for the story."

He squeezed Thomas's wrist just a little harder. For an old man, he was very strong.

"Story," Claus muttered. "I wish I could use you for the story. But times have changed."

"Is that what the elves were alluding to? Someone else has caught you?"

"You'll kick yourself when I tell you." Claus grinned. His teeth were pointed, almost fanged. Thomas wondered how he ever found this face pleasant.

"Clement Moore," Thomas said softly.

"Twas the Night Before Christmas. Same day, different year. Different century." Claus tilted his head, looking thoughtful. "Didn't have computers then. We weren't as accurate in knowing who'd be home and who wouldn't be. *He* had children I could threaten. You keep losing your fiancées."

"You know that?"

"My mind is full of useless information, all of it relating to goodness or badness. You'd think magic would be great—and it probably would if someone got the stuff of stories, you know, the ability to make things disappear, being able to fly things across a room. But no. I get stupid talents. Seeing people while they sleep. They lay in one position for a while, sigh, and roll over. Nothing exciting there. And the naughty and nice stuff? Good for the occasional blackmail, but nothing more."

Claus rolled his tiny eyes. Thomas strained to hear those sirens. But he couldn't, not yet. How good were those elven ears?

"I'd like to pat you on the head and tell you to write a nice poem, filled with *my* lies, of course, and a little bit of the truth," Claus said. "But these days, the myth-making machine is self-generating. Who'd've known what a boon television would be?"

"Who'd've known?" Thomas asked. He swallowed, wondering if he could shake himself free, and get out those double doors before the Jolly Old Elf caught him. Probably. It would be worth a try.

"So," Claus said, "I think I'll just let you go."

Thomas had been concentrating so much on escaping that he almost missed what Claus said. "What?"

"I'm letting you go." Claus dropped Thomas's wrist like it contaminated him. "Toddle on."

"But they'll catch you."

"No, they won't," Claus said, going to the storage area, dropping and locking the door.

"I'll tell," Thomas said.

"Of course you will." Claus grinned. "But who's going to believe you?"

***

NO ONE, IT TURNED OUT. Not the cops who showed up, only to be greeted by the big man himself ("Sorry to bother you, officers. We got an early morning shipment and this man was worried."), not Thomas's old editor ("Tom, I say this only as a friend. Counseling. Lots of counseling.") and especially not fiancée number three ("Don't ever call me again. Ever!").

In the end, there was nothing he could do. Oh, he called and reported a few break-ins before they occurred, but that only got him brought him to the attention of the police –and not in a good way. And then he tried to warn potential victims, which only made his police surveillance worse. He soon figured that if he continued along this path, he would soon be arrested for the crimes himself.

And to make matters worse, every January, he got a postcard from Florida—that year's Santa postcard, which always had the happy *Wish You Were Here!* on the front. On the back was just a scrawled number.

That first year he had no idea what the number meant. But the second year, after he mapped the robberies, he knew.

Total profits, after expenses, of course. Never less than ten million dollars. Tax free.

The old guy could have quit years ago. But he didn't. He wasn't doing it for the money. He was addicted to the belief.

And Thomas, whom everyone doubted, understood why.

Substitutions

SILAS SAT AT THE BLACKJACK TABLE, a plastic glass of whiskey in his left hand, and a small pile of hundred dollar chips in his right. His banjo rested against his boot, the embroidered strap wrapped around his calf. He had a pair of aces to the dealer's six, so he split them—a thousand dollars riding on each—and watched as she covered them with the expected tens.

He couldn't lose. He'd been trying to all night.

The casino was empty except for five gambling addicts hunkered over the blackjack table, one old woman playing slots with the rhythm of an assembly worker, and one young man in black leather who was getting drunk at the casino's sorry excuse for a bar. The employees showed no sign of holiday cheer: no happy holiday pins, no little Santa hats, only the stark black and white of their uniforms against the casino's fading glitter.

He had chosen the Paradise because it was one of the few remaining fifties-style casinos in Nevada, still thick with flocked wallpaper and cigarette smoke, craps tables worn by dice and elbows, and the roulette wheel creaking with age. It was also only a few hours from Reno, and in thirty hours, he would have to make the tortuous drive up there. Along the way, he would visit an old man who had a bad heart; a young girl who would cross the road at the wrong time and meet an on-coming semi; and a baby boy who was born with his lungs not yet fully formed. Silas also suspected a few surprises along the way; nothing was ever as it seemed any longer. Life was moving too fast, even for him.

But he had Christmas Eve and Christmas Day off, the two days he had chosen when he had been picked to work Nevada 150 years before. In those days, he would go home for Christmas, see his friends, spend time with his family. His parents welcomed him, even though they didn't see him for most of the year. He felt like a boy again, like someone cherished and loved, instead of the drifter he had become.

All of that stopped in 1878. December 26th, 1878. He wasn't yet sophisticated enough to know that the day was a holiday in England. Boxing Day. Not quite appropriate, but close.

He had to take his father that day. The old man had looked pale and tired throughout the holiday, but no one thought it serious. When he took to his bed Christmas night, everyone had simply thought him tired from the festivities.

It was only after midnight, when Silas got his orders, that he knew what was coming next. He begged off—

something he had never tried before (he wasn't even sure who he had been begging with)—but had received the feeling (that was all he ever got: a firm feeling, so strong he couldn't avoid it) that if he didn't do it, death would come another way—from Idaho or California or New Mexico. It would come another way, his father would be in agony for days, and the end, when it came, would be uglier than it had to be.

Silas had taken his banjo to the old man's room. His mother slept on her side, like she always had, her back to his father. His father's eyes had opened, and he knew. Somehow he knew.

They always did.

Silas couldn't remember what he said. Something—a bit of an apology, maybe, or just an explanation: *You always wanted to know what I did.* And then, the moment. First he touched his father's forehead, clammy with the illness that would claim him, and then Silas said, "You wanted to know why I carry the banjo," and strummed.

But the sound did not soothe his father like it had so many before him. As his spirit rose, his body struggled to hold it, and he looked at Silas with such a mix of fear and betrayal that Silas still saw it whenever he thought of his father.

The old man died, but not quickly and not easily, and Silas tried to resign, only to get sent to the place that passed for headquarters, a small shack that resembled an out-of-the-way railroad terminal. There, a man who looked no more than thirty but who had to be three hundred or more, told him the more that he complained, the longer his service would last.

Silas never complained again, and he had been on the job for 150 years. Almost 55,000 days spent in the service of Death, with only Christmas Eve and Christmas off, tainted holidays for a man in a tainted position.

He scooped up his winnings, piled them on his already-high stack of chips, and then placed his next bet. The dealer had just given him a queen and a jack when a boy sat down beside him.

"Boy" wasn't entirely accurate. He was old enough to get into the casino. But he had rain on his cheap jacket, and hair that hadn't been cut in a long time. IPod headphones stuck out of his breast pocket, and he had a cell phone against his hip the way that old sheriffs used to wear their guns.

His hands were callused and the nails had dirt beneath them. He looked tired, and a little frightened.

He watched as the dealer busted, then set chips in front of Silas and the four remaining players. Silas swept the chips into his stack, grabbed five of the hundred dollar chips, and placed the bet.

The dealer swept her hand along the semi-circle, silently asking the players to place their bets.

"You Silas?" the boy asked. He hadn't put any money on the table or placed any chips before him.

Silas sighed. Only once before had someone interrupted his Christmas festivities—if festivities was what the last century plus could be called.

The dealer peered at the boy. "You gonna play?"

The boy looked at her, startled. He didn't seem to know what to say.

"I got it." Silas put twenty dollars in chips in front of the boy.

"I don't know…"

"Just do what I tell you," Silas said.

The woman dealt, face-up. Silas got an ace. The boy, an eight. The woman dealt herself a ten. Then she went around again. Silas got his twenty-one—his weird holiday luck holding—but the boy got another eight.

"Split them," Silas said.

The boy looked at him, his fear almost palpable.

Silas sighed again, then grabbed another twenty in chips, and placed it next to the boy's first twenty.

"Jeez, mister, that's a lot of money," the boy whispered.

"Splitting," Silas said to the dealer.

She separated the cards and placed the bets behind them. Then she dealt the boy two cards—a ten and another eight.

The boy looked at Silas. Looked like the boy had peculiar luck as well.

"Split again," Silas said, more to the dealer than to the boy. He added the bet, let her separate the cards, and watched as she dealt the boy two more tens. Three eighteens. Not quite as good as Silas's twenties to twenty-ones, but just as statistically uncomfortable.

The dealer finished her round, then dealt herself a three, then a nine, busting again. She paid in order.

When she reached the boy, she set sixty dollars in chips before him, each in its own twenty dollar pile.

"Take it," Silas said.

"It's yours," the boy said, barely speaking above a whisper. "I gave it to you."

"I don't gamble," the boy said.

"Well, for someone who doesn't gamble, you did pretty well. Take your winnings."

The boy looked at them as if they'd bite him. "I…"

"Are you leaving them for the next round?" the dealer asked.

The boy's eyes widened. He was clearly horrified at the very thought. With shaking fingers, he collected the chips, then leaned into Silas. The boy smelled of sweat and wet wool.

"Can I talk to you?" he whispered.

Silas nodded, then cashed in his chips. He'd racked up ten thousand dollars in three hours. He wasn't even having fun at it any more. He liked losing, felt that it was appropriate—part of the game, part of his life—but the losses had become fewer and farther between the more he played.

The more he lived. A hundred years ago, there were women and a few adopted children. But watching them grow old, helping three of them die, had taken the desire out of that too.

"Mr. Silas," the boy whispered.

"If you're not going to bet," the dealer said, "please move so someone can have your seats."

People had gathered behind Silas, and he hadn't even noticed. He really didn't care tonight. Normally, he would have noticed anyone around him—noticed who they were, how and when they would die.

"Come on," he said, gathering the bills the dealer had given him. The boy's eyes went to the money like a hungry man's went to food. His one-hundred-and-twenty dollars remained on the table, and Silas had to remind him to pick it up.

The boy used a forefinger and a thumb to carry it, as if it would burn him.

"At least put it in your pocket," Silas snapped.

"But it's yours," the boy said.

"It's a damn gift. Appreciate it."

The boy blinked, then stuffed the money into the front of his unwashed jeans. Silas led him around banks and banks of slot machines, all pinging and ponging and making little musical come-ons, to the steakhouse in the back.

The steakhouse was the reason Silas came back year after year. The place opened at five, closed at three a.m., and served the best steaks in Vegas. They weren't arty or too small. One big slab of meat, expensive cut, charred on the outside and red as Christmas on the inside. Beside the steak they served french-fried onions, and sides that no self-respecting Strip restaurant would prepare—creamed corn, au gratin potatoes, popovers—the kind of stuff that Silas always associated with the modern Las Vegas—modern, to him, meaning 1950s-1960s Vegas. Sin city. A place for grown-ups to gamble and smoke and drink and have affairs. The Vegas of Sinatra and the mob, not the Vegas of Steve Wynn and his ilk, who prettified everything and made it all seem upscale and oh-so-right.

Silas still worked Vegas a lot more than any other Nevada city, which made sense, considering how many millions of people lived there now, but millions of people lived all over. Even sparsely populated Nevada, one of the least populated states in the Union, had ten full-time Death employees. They tried to unionize a few years ago, but Silas, with the most seniority, refused to join. Then they tried to limit the routes—one would get Reno, another Sparks, another Elko and that region, and a few would split Vegas—but Silas wouldn't agree to that either.

He loved the travel part of the job. It was the only part he still liked, the ability to go from place to place to place, see the changes, understand how time affected everything.

Everything except him.

The maitre d sat them in the back, probably because of the boy. Even in this modern era, where people wore blue jeans to funerals, this steakhouse preferred its customers in a suit and tie.

The booth was made of wood and rose so high that Silas couldn't see anything but the boy and the table across from them. A single lamp reflected against the wall, revealing cloth napkins and real silver utensils.

The boy stared at them with the same kind of fear he had shown at the blackjack table. "I can't—."

The maître d gave them leather-bound menus, said something about a special, and then handed Silas a wine list. Silas ordered a bottle of burgundy. He didn't know a lot about wines, just that the more expensive ones tasted a lot better than the rest of them. So he ordered the most expensive burgundy on the menu.

The maître d nodded crisply, almost militarily, and then left. The boy leaned forward.

"I can't stay. I'm your substitute."

Silas smiled. A waiter came by with a bread basket—hard rolls, still warm—and relish trays filled with sliced carrots, celery, and radishes, and candied beets, things people now would call old-fashioned.

Modern, to him. Just as modern as always.

The boy squirmed, his jeans squeaking on the leather booth.

"I know," Silas said. "You'll be fine."

"I got—

"A big one, probably," Silas said. "It's Christmas Eve. Traffic, right? A shooting in a church? Too many suicides?"

"No," the boy said, distressed. "Not like that."

"When's it scheduled for?" Silas asked. He really wanted his dinner, and he didn't mind sharing it. The boy looked like he needed a good meal.

"Tonight," the boy said. "No specific time. See?"

He put a crumpled piece of paper between them, but Silas didn't pick it up.

"Means you have until midnight," Silas said. "It's only seven. You can eat."

"They said at orientation—

Silas had forgotten; they all got orientation now. The expectations of generations. He'd been thrown into the pool feet first, fumbling his way for six months before someone told him that he could actually ask questions.

"—the longer you wait, the more they suffer."

Silas glanced at the paper. "If it's big, it's a surprise. They won't suffer. They'll just finish when you get there. That's all."

The boy bit his lip. "How do you know?"

Because he'd had big. He'd had grisly. He'd had disgusting. He'd overseen more deaths than the boy could imagine.

The head waiter arrived, took Silas's order, and then turned to the boy.

"I don't got money," the boy said.

"You have one-hundred-and-twenty dollars," Silas said. "But I'm buying, so don't worry."

The boy opened the menu, saw the prices, and closed it again. He shook his head.

The waiter started to leave when Silas stopped him. "Give him what I'm having. Medium well."

Since the kid didn't look like he ate many steaks, he wouldn't like his rare. Rare was an acquired taste, just like burgundy wine and the cigar that Silas wished he could light up. Not everything in the modern era was an improvement.

"You don't have to keep paying for me," the kid said.

Silas waved the waiter away, then leaned back. The back of the booth, made of wood, was rigid against his spine. "After a while in this business," he said, "money is all you have."

The kid bit his lower lip. "Look at the paper. Make sure I'm not screwing up. Please."

But Silas didn't look.

"You're supposed to handle all of this on your own," Silas said gently.

"I know," the boy said. "I know. But this one, he's scary. And I don't think anything I do will make it right."

***

AFTER HE FINISHED HIS STEAK and had his first sip of coffee, about the time he would have lit up his cigar, Silas picked up the paper. The boy had devoured the steak like he hadn't eaten in weeks. He ate all the bread and everything from his relish tray.

He was very, very new.

Silas wondered how someone that young had gotten into the death business, but he was determined not to ask. It would be some variation on his own story. Silas had begged for the life of his wife who should have died in the delivery of their second child. Begged, and begged, and begged, and somehow, in his befogged state, he actually saw the woman whom he then called the Angel of Death.

Now he knew better—none of them were angels, just working stiffs waiting for retirement—but then, she had seemed perfect and terrifying, all at the same time.

He'd asked for his wife, saying he didn't want to raise his daughters alone.

The angel had tilted her head. "Would you die for her?"

"Of course," Silas said.

"Leaving her to raise the children alone?" the angel asked.

His breath caught. "Is that my only choice?"

She shrugged, as if she didn't care. Later, when he reflected, he realized she didn't know.

"Yes," he said into her silence. "She would raise better people than I will. She's good. I'm…not."

He wasn't bad, he later realized, just lost, as so many were. His wife had been a god-fearing woman with strict ideas about morality. She had raised two marvelous girls, who became two strong women, mothers of large broods who all went on to do good works.

In that, he hadn't been wrong.

But his wife hadn't remarried either, and she had cried for him for the rest of her days.

They had lived in Texas. He had made his bargain, got assigned Nevada, and had to swear never to head east, not while his wife and children lived. His parents saw him, but they couldn't tell anyone. They thought he ran out on his wife and children, and oddly, they had supported him in it.

Remnants of his family still lived. Great-grandchildren generations removed. He still couldn't head east, and he no longer wanted to.

Silas touched the paper and it burned his fingers. A sign, a warning, a remembrance that he wasn't supposed to work these two days.

Two days out of an entire year.

He slid the paper back to the boy. "I can't open it. I'm not allowed. You tell me."

So the boy did.

And Silas, in wonderment that they had sent a rookie into a situation a veteran might not be able to handle, settled his tab, took the boy by the arm, and led him into the night.

***

EVERY CITY HAS POCKETS OF EVIL. Vegas had fewer than most, despite the things the television lied about. So many people worked in law enforcement or security, so many others were bonded so that they could work in casinos or high-end jewelry stores or banks that Vegas's serious crime was lower than most comparable cities of its size.

Silas appreciated that. Most of the time, it meant that the deaths he attended in Vegas were natural or easy or just plain silly. He got a lot of silly deaths in that city. Some he even found time to laugh over.

But not this one.

As they drove from the very edge of town, past the rows and rows of similar houses, past the stink and desperation of complete poverty, he finally asked, "How long've you been doing this?"

"Six months," the boy said softly, as if that were forever.

Silas looked at him, looked at the young face reflecting the Christmas lights that filled the neighborhood, and shook his head. "All substitutes?"

The boy shrugged. "They didn't have any open routes."

"What about the guy you replaced?"

"He'd been subbing, waiting to retire. They say you could retire too, but you show no signs of it. Working too hard, even for a younger man."

He wasn't older. He was the same age he had been when his wife struggled with her labor—a breach birth that would be no problem in 2006, but had been deadly if not handled right in 1856. The midwife's hands hadn't been clean—not that anyone knew better in those days—and the infection had started even before the baby got turned.

He shuddered, that night alive in him. The night he'd made his bargain.

"I don't work hard," he said. "I work less than I did when I started."

The boy looked at him, surprised. "Why don't you retire?"

"And do what?" Silas asked. He hadn't planned to speak up. He normally shrugged off that question.

"I dunno," the boy said. "Relax. Live off your savings. Have a family again."

They could all have families again when they retired. Families and a good, rich life, albeit short. Silas would age when he retired. He would age and have no special powers. He would watch a new wife die in childbirth and not be able to see his former colleague sitting beside the bed. He would watch his children squirm after a car accident, blood on their faces, knowing that they would live poorly if they lived at all, and not be able to find out the future from the death dealer hovering near the scene.

Better to continue. Better to keep this half-life, this half-future, time without end.

"Families are overrated," Silas said. They look at you with betrayal and loss when you do what was right.

But the boy didn't know that yet. He didn't know a lot.

"You ever get scared?" the boy asked.

"Of what?" Silas asked. Then gave the standard answer. "They can't kill you. They can't harm you. You just move from place to place, doing your job. There's nothing to be scared of."

The boy grunted, sighed, and looked out the window.

Silas knew what he had asked, and hadn't answered it. Of course he got scared. All the time. And not of dying—even though he still wasn't sure what happened to the souls he freed. He wasn't scared of that, or of the people he occasionally faced down, the drug addicts with their knives, the gangsters with their guns, the wannabe outlaws with blood all over their hands.

No, the boy had asked about the one thing to be afraid of, the one thing they couldn't change.

Was he scared of being alone? Of remaining alone, for the rest of his days? Was he scared of being unknown and nearly invisible, having no ties and no dreams?

It was too late to be scared of that.

He'd lived it. He lived it every single day.

***

THE HOUSE WAS ONE OF THOSE square adobe things that filled Vegas. It was probably pink in the sunlight. In the half-light that passed for nighttime in this perpetually alive city, it looked gray and foreboding.

The bars on the windows—standard in this neighborhood—didn't help.

Places like this always astounded him. They seemed so normal, so incorruptible, just another building on another street, like all the other buildings on all the other streets. Sometimes he got to go into those buildings. Very few of them were different from what he expected. Oh, the art changed or the furniture. The smells differed—sometimes unwashed diapers, sometimes perfume, sometimes the heavy scent of meals eaten long ago—but the rest remained the same: the television in the main room, the kitchen with its square table (sometimes decorated with flowers, sometimes nothing but trash), the double bed in the second bedroom down the hall, the one with its own shower and toilet. The room across from the main bathroom was sometimes an office, sometimes a den, sometimes a child's bedroom. If it was a child's bedroom, there were pictures on the wall, studio portraits from the local mall, done up in cheap frames, showing the passing years. The pictures were never straight, and always dusty, except for the most recent, hung with pride in the only remaining empty space.

He had a hunch this house would have none of those things. If anything, it would have an overly neat interior. The television would be in the kitchen or the bedroom or both. The front room would have a sofa set designed for looks, not for comfort. And one of the rooms would be blocked off, maybe even marked private, and in it, he would find (if he looked) trophies of a kind that made even his cast-iron stomach turn.

These houses had no attic. Most didn't have a basement. So the scene would be the garage. The car would be parked outside of it, blocking the door, and the neighbors would assume that the garage was simply a workspace—not that far off, if the truth be told.

He'd been to places like this before. More times than he wanted to think about, especially in the smaller communities out in the desert, the communities that had no names, or once had a name and did no longer. The communities sometimes made up of cheap trailers and empty storefronts, with a whorehouse a few miles off the main highway, and a casino in the center of town, a casino so old it made the one that the boy found him in look like it had been built just the week before.

He hated these jobs. He wasn't sure what made him come with the boy. A moment of compassion? The prospect of yet another long Christmas Eve with nothing to punctuate it except the bong-bong of nearby slots?

He couldn't go to church any more. It didn't feel right, with as many lives as he had taken. He couldn't go to church or listen to the singing or look at the families and wonder which of them he'd be standing beside in thirty years.

Maybe he belonged here more than the boy did. Maybe he belonged here more than anyone else.

They parked a block away, not because anyone would see their car—if asked, hours later, the neighbors would deny seeing anything to do with Silas or the boy. Maybe they never saw, maybe their memories vanished. Silas had never been clear on that either.

As they got out, Silas asked, "What do you use?"

The boy reached into the breast pocket. For a moment, Silas thought he'd remove the iPod, and Silas wasn't sure how a device that used headphones would work. Then the boy removed a harmonica—expensive, the kind sold at high-end music stores.

"You play that before all this?" Silas asked.

The boy nodded. "They got me a better one, though."

Silas's banjo had been all his own. They'd let him take it, and nothing else. The banjo, the clothes he wore that night, his hat.

He had different clothes now. He never wore a hat. But his banjo was the same as it had always been—new and pure with a sound that he still loved.

It was in the trunk. He doubted it could get stolen, but he took precautions just in case.

He couldn't bring it on this job. This wasn't his job. He'd learned the hard way that the banjo didn't work except in assigned cases. When he'd wanted to help, to put someone out of their misery, to step in where another death dealer had failed, he couldn't. He could only watch, like normal people did, and hope that things got better, even though he knew it wouldn't.

The boy clutched the harmonica in his right hand. The dry desert air was cold. Silas could see his breath. The tourists down on the Strip, with their short skirts and short sleeves, probably felt betrayed by the normal winter chill. He wished he were there with them, instead of walking through this quiet neighborhood, filled with dark houses, dirt-ridden yards, and silence.

So much silence. You'd think there'd be at least one barking dog.

When they reached the house, the boy headed to the garage, just like Silas expected. A car was parked on the road—a 1980s sedan that looked like it had seen better days. In the driveway, a brand-new van with tinted windows, custom-made for bad deeds.

In spite of himself, Silas shuddered.

The boy stopped outside and steeled himself, then he looked at Silas with sadness in his eyes. Silas nodded. The boy extended a hand—Silas couldn't get in without the boy's momentary magic—and then they were inside, near the stench of old gasoline, urine, and fear.

The kids sat in a dimly lit corner, chained together like the slaves on ships in the 19th century. The windows were covered with dirty cardboard, the concrete floor was empty except for stains as old as time. It felt bad in here, a recognizable bad, one Silas had encountered before.

The boy was shaking. He wasn't out of place here, his old wool jacket and his dirty jeans making him a cousin to the kids on the floor. Silas had a momentary flash: they were homeless. Runaways, lost, children without borders, without someone looking for them.

"You've been here before," Silas whispered to the boy and the boy's eyes filled with tears.

Been here, negotiated here, moved on here—didn't quite die, but no longer quite lived—and for who? A group of kids like this one? A group that had somehow escaped, but hadn't reported what had happened?

Then he felt the chill grow worse. Of course they hadn't reported it. Who would believe them? A neat homeowner kidnaps a group of homeless kids for his own personal playthings, and the cops believe the kids? Kids who steal and sell drugs and themselves just for survival.

People like the one who owned this house were cautious. They were smart. They rarely got caught unless they went public with letters or phone calls or both.

They had to prepare for contingencies like losing a plaything now and then. They probably had all the answers planned.

A side door opened. It was attached to the house. The man who came in was everything Silas had expected—white, thin, balding, a bit too intense.

What surprised Silas was the look the man gave him. Measuring, calculating.

Pleased.

The man wasn't supposed to see Silas or the boy. Not until the last moment.

Not until the end.

Silas had heard that some of these creatures could see the death dealers. A few of Silas's colleagues speculated that these men continued to kill so that they could continue to see death in all its forms, collecting images the way they collected trophies.

After seeing the momentary victory in that man's eyes, Silas believed it.

The man picked up the kid at the end of the chain. Too weak to stand, the kid staggered a bit, then had to lean into the man.

"You have to beat me," the man said to Silas. "I slice her first, and you have to leave."

The boy was still shivering. The man hadn't noticed him. The man thought Silas was here for him, not the boy. Silas had no powers, except the ones that humans normally had—not on this night, and not in this way.

If he were here alone, he'd start playing, and praying he'd get the right one. If there was a right one. He couldn't tell. They all seemed to have the mark of death over them.

No wonder the boy needed him.

It was a fluid situation, one that could go in any direction.

"Start playing," Silas said under his breath.

But the man heard him, not the boy. The man pulled the kid's head back, exposing a smooth white throat with the heartbeat visible in a vein.

"Play!" Silas shouted, and ran forward, shoving the man aside, hoping that would be enough.

It saved the girl's neck, for a moment anyway. She fell, and landed on the other kid next to her. The kid moved away, as if proximity to her would cause the kid to die.

The boy started blowing on his harmonica. The notes were faint, barely notes, more like bleats of terror.

The man laughed. He saw the boy now. "So you're back to rob me again," he said.

The boy's playing grew wispier.

"Ignore him," Silas said to the boy.

"Who're you? His coach?" The man approached him. "I know your rules. I destroy you, I get to take your place."

The steak rolled in Silas's stomach. The man was half right. He destroyed Silas, and he would get a chance to take the job. He destroyed both of them, and he would get the job, by old magic not new. Silas had forgotten this danger. No wonder these creatures liked to see death— what better for them than to be the facilitator for the hundreds of people who died in Nevada every day.

The man brandished his knife. "Lessee," he said. "What do I do? Destroy the instrument, deface the man. Right? And send him to hell."

Get him fired, Silas fought. It wasn't really hell, although it seemed like it. He became a ghost, existing forever, but not allowed to interact with anything. He was fired. He lost the right to die.

The man reached for the harmonica. Silas shoved again.

"Play!" Silas shouted.

And miraculously, the boy played. "Home on the Range," a silly song for these circumstances, but probably the first tune the boy had ever learned. He played it with spirit as he backed away from the fight.

But the kids weren't rebelling. They sat on the cold concrete floor, already half dead, probably tortured into submission. If they didn't rise up and kill this monster, no one would.

Silas looked at the boy. Tears streamed down his face, and he nodded toward the kids. Souls hovered above them, as if they couldn't decide whether or not to leave.

Damn the ones in charge: they'd sent the kid here as his final test. Could he take the kind of lives he had given his life for? Was he that strong?

The man reached for the harmonica again, and this time Silas grabbed his knife. It was heavier than Silas expected. He had never wielded a real instrument of death. His banjo eased people into forever. It didn't force them out of their lives a moment too early.

The boy kept playing and the man—the creature—laughed. One of the kids looked up, and Silas thought the kid was staring straight at the boy.

Only a moment, then. Only a moment to decide.

Silas shoved the knife into the man's belly. It went in deep, and the man let out an oof of pain. He stumbled, reached for the knife, and then glared at Silas.

Silas hadn't killed him, maybe hadn't even mortally wounded him. No soul appeared above him, and even these creatures had souls—dark and tainted as they were.

The boy's playing broke in places as if he were trying to catch his breath. The kid at the end of the chain, the girl, managed to get up. She looked at the knife, then at the man, then around the room. She couldn't see Silas or the boy.

Which was good.

The man was pulling on the knife. He would get it free in a moment. He would use it, would destroy these children, the ones no one cared about except the boy who was here to take their souls.

The girl kicked the kid beside her. "Stand up," she said.

The kid looked at her, bleary. Silas couldn't tell if these kids were male or female. He wasn't sure it mattered.

"Stand up," the girl said again.

In a rattle of chains, the kid did. The man didn't notice. He was working the knife, grunting as he tried to dislodge it. Silas stepped back, wondering if he had already interfered too much.

The music got louder, more intense, almost violent. The girl stood beside the man and stared at him for a moment.

He raised his head, saw her, and grinned.

Then she reached down with that chain, wrapped it around his neck and pulled. "Help me," she said to the others. "Help me."

The music became a live thing, wrapping them all, filling the smelly garage, and reaching deep, deep into the darkness. The soul did rise up—half a soul, broken and burned. It looked at Silas, then flared at the boy, who—bless him—didn't stop playing.

Then the soul floated toward the growing darkness in the corner, a blackness Silas had seen only a handful of times before, a blackness that felt as cold and dark as any empty desert night, and somehow much more permanent.

The music faded. The girl kept pulling, until another kid, farther down the line, convinced her to let go.

"We have to find the key," the other kid—a boy—said.

"On the wall," a third kid said. "Behind the electric box."

They shuffled as a group toward the box. They walked through Silas, and he felt them, alive and vibrant. For a moment, he worried that he had been fired, but he knew he had too many years for that. Too many years of perfect service—and he hadn't killed the man. He had just injured him, took away the threat to the boy.

That was allowed, just barely.

No wonder the boy had brought him. No wonder the boy had asked him if he was scared. Not of being alone or being lonely. But of certain jobs, of the things now asked of them as the no-longer-quite-human beings that they were.

Silas turned to the boy. His face was shiny with tears, but his eyes were clear. He stuffed the harmonica back into his breast pocket.

"You knew he'd beat you without me," Silas said.

The boy nodded.

"You knew this wasn't a substitution. You would have had this job, even without me."

"It's not cheating to bring in help," the boy said.

"But it's nearly impossible to find it," Silas said. "How did you find me?"

"It's Christmas Eve," the boy said. "Everyone knows where you'd be."

Everyone. His colleagues. People on the job. The only folks who even knew his name any more.

Silas sighed. The boy reached out with his stubby dirty hand. Silas took it, and then, suddenly, they were out of that fetid garage. They stood next to the van and watched as the cardboard came off one of the windows, as glass shattered outward.

Kids, homeless kids, injured and alone, poured out of that window like water.

"Thanks," the boy said. "I can't tell you how much it means."

But Silas knew. The boy didn't yet, but Silas did. When he retired—no longer if. When—this boy would see him again. This boy would take him, gently and with some kind of majestic harmonica music, to a beyond Silas could not imagine.

The boy waved at him, and joined the kids, heading into the dark Vegas night. Those kids couldn't see him, but they had to know he was there, like a guardian angel, saving them from horrors that would haunt their dreams for the rest of their lives.

Silas watched them go. Then he headed in the opposite direction, toward his car. What had those kids seen? The man—the creature—with his knife out, raving at nothing. Then stumbling backwards, once, twice, the second time with a knife in his belly. They'd think that he tripped, that he stabbed himself. None of them had seen Silas or the boy.

They wouldn't for another sixty years.

If they were lucky.

The neighborhood remained dark, although a dog barked in the distance. His car was cold. Cold and empty.

He let himself in, started it, warmed his fingers against the still-hot air blowing out of the vents. Only a few minutes gone. A few minutes to take away a nasty, horrible lifetime. He wondered what was in the rest of these houses, and hoped he'd never have to find out.

The clock on the dash read 10:45. As he drove out of the neighborhood, he passed a small adobe church. Outside, candles burned in candleholders made of baked sand. Almost like the churches of his childhood.

Almost, but not quite.

He watched the people thread inside. They wore fancy clothing—dresses on the women, suits on the men, the children dressing like their parents, faces alive with anticipation.

They believed in something.

They had hope.

He wondered if hope was something a man could recapture, if it came with time, relaxation, and the slow inevitable march toward death.

He wondered, if he retired, whether he could spend his Christmas Eves inside, smelling the mix of incense and candle wax, the evergreen boughs, and the light dusting of ladies' perfume.

He wondered…

Then shook his head.

And drove back to the casino, to spend the rest of his time off in peace.

Nutball Season

*I*N MY BUSINESS, NUTBALL SEASON starts on Halloween, and goes to about Christmas. Oh, you get your occasional Friday-the-thirteenth run on the precinct, and you gotta pray you get every full moon off, but the real serious wackos don't seem to surface until about the last week in October, and they don't disappear until New Year's Day. What they do the rest of the year, I haven't the slightest. But up until then, they're harassing me and mine, or folks just like us all over the country.

Every year, I got my favorite nut story. But last year's I don't talk about much. Because I ain't sure exactly who the nut is, me or the geezer what started it all.

You see, he walked into the stationhouse a shade before midnight on December twenty-third, wearing a red Santa suit, and looking pasty and tired, that kinda tired we all get when we pull too many shifts in a row. The house was empty that night. The desk sarge was handling some crisis, the dispatch was doing his nails, for godsake, and most everyone else was either at their own homes or doing their beats.

Me, I was at my desk. I'd stopped in the precinct after a collar to finish up some paperwork before going home to macaroni, cheese and tuna, my specialty. Not that I minded. It was better than Cindy Lou's meatloaf surprise, which I missed even less than I missed her. So I wasn't really in a hurry to leave—even though soaking up the camaraderie of the stationhouse at that time of night was kinda like trying to sleep in a rooms-by-the-hour motel.

The old guy came in as I was typing the last part of my report. He sat down in the metal chair before my desk, leaned over the files like he owned the place and said, "Excuse me."

I held up my hand, signaling he should wait until I was finished, hoping someone else would come into the barren house and the old guy would trot off to them. No luck.

"Excuse me," he said again. "Where do I go to file a complaint?"

I knew I wasn't gonna get rid of him as easy as I wanted so I said, "A complaint about what?"

"Mrs. Billings. She plans to shoot me if I land on her roof tomorrow night."

Now to understand that sentence, you had to know that the next night was Christmas Eve. And since it was Christmas Eve, and he was an elderly guy with a long white beard dressed all in red, it was pretty clear who he was gonna impersonate.

At least, that was how I thought of it at that moment. But I wasn't being quick on the uptake. I didn't think about the implications of asking this guy a question. Which I did.

"Does this Mrs. Billings have a child?"

"Well, of course," the old guy said in his precise way, and I realized then and there that I should have kept my mouth shut because I was buying into his fantasy.

Of course, my mouth hadn't stayed shut, and now I was in deep, and I tried to fix it, I really did. I told him, you know, that maybe he could wait a day or stay off the roof or just plain get outta town.

He looked at me like it was sixth grade again and he was Sister Mary Catherine trying to explain Algebra.

"You simply do not understand," he said. "I cannot stay out of town. I must come, and I must arrive on that night. I cannot change that. Too many children will be disappointed."

"Listen, bub," I said. "I know it's Christmas and all, but you know, kids really can't tell time. They won't notice if Santa arrives on Christmas Eve or the day after."

"They'll notice," he said in that precise way of his. It was his manner of speaking that really got me to look at him. He didn't sound like he was from around here.

I know, I know, I don't exactly sound Upstate either, but you can tell I do belong in New York. This guy sounded kinda English, but kinda like Katherine Hepburn too. You know. Cultured.

And the voice didn't quite suit him either. I mean how do you expect a guy dressed like Santa to sound? Me, I'd think all deep voiced and jolly. But no one'd think jolly about this guy. They wouldn't even think fat. This guy was big, but he was all muscle. His eyes weren't twinkling. They were that hard steel gray that some beat cops get after too many long days. And his beard wasn't snowy white. It was a yellowish silver, the yellow probably being tobacco stains from the pipe clenched tightly in his thin mouth.

"Take it from me," I said to him, "when I was a kid, there was this guy next door who worked for PhilcoFord. This was in the days when companies really cared about their workers, you know? And his guy's kid, he was my age. The company Santa drops by every year, not just to this guy's house, but to ours too, and he always came on a Sunday, but I don't really notice, you know—"

"Not until thirteen year-old Michael Trent pointed it out to you. I know," the geezer said. "He got coal in his stocking that year."

The hair on the back of my neck stood out. The moment was a bit too *Miracle on 34th Street* for me. Now, there coulda been a thousand explanations for him knowing that—I mean I told that story a hundred times—but how he knew he'd get me that night, I couldn't figure.

I decided to ignore the geezer's last comment.

"Anyway," I said. "The point is—"

"That the children don't notice, but they do. They have an internal sense of what's right and what's not, particularly when it comes to Christmas. And that's at the heart of my dilemma."

"How's that?" I ask.

"She has a child. A boy of three. He's a good boy, too, and doesn't ask for much. Her neighbors' children have all grown, and they visit their grandchildren on the holidays, so her son is the only child on the block. Logic dictates that I skip the house, but I simply cannot. In the centuries that I have been doing this work—"

Those hairs rose again. I was gonna have to get them trimmed.

"—I haven't skipped a single child. At least, not a single child who met the criteria."

I didn't want to ask about criteria. I didn't want to know the details. I was sure the old guy would give them to me.

"Mr.—"

"Kringle."

"Yeah, right. Listen, we can visit the lady, ask her to stop threatening you, but without proof or an incident there ain't much we could do. Now you can get yourself a lawyer, and have some judge order her to stay away from you, but even that won't do no good when you go visit her house, don't you see? Maybe there's some other way you can get the presents to the kid."

He stared at me for a moment, and I got the sense, even though he was too polite to say it, that I just didn't get it.

"I have proof," he said softly.

"You do?" For all his complaints against this woman, he never once said nothing about proof. "Well lessee it."

He gave me photocopies—dozens of them—all letters, all from different children, all return addresses right here in our little burg. As he passed the copies to me, he stuck his finger on the top letter and hit it with such force that the sound echoed through the empty precinct.

"Right—" tap "—there."

I glanced at the top letter. It was from a nine-year-old girl. It said that she heard Mrs. Prudence Billings say she'd shoot Santa if he landed on her roof. The little girl, she was writing to warn Santa, and to tell him it was okay if he skipped her this year because she'd rather he'd be safe.

The kid was probably trying to guarantee free presents for life.

Then I thumbed through the letters. They were all versions of the same thing: the kids had heard this Prudence Billings say she'd shoot Santa.

What a great woman. Jeez. What was she doing telling children them things?

"You need a lawyer, Mister," I said, handing the letters back to him.

"But that doesn't solve my dilemma," he said. "I need to go to her house."

"Like I said, get someone else to deliver," and I leaned back in my chair thinking about her poor kid. Imagine having a mom who didn't let you believe in Santa, who didn't let you have that one night when you thought anything was possible, when you actually believed some fat bastard who had flying reindeer could squeeze himself into a space barely wide enough for a broom and give you your heart's desire?

"I can't get someone else to deliver," the geezer said, sounding kinda forlorn. "This isn't a task that can be handed from person to person."

I was feeling a bit bad now. I mean, everyone's entitled to their own delusions if they didn't hurt nobody. But the guy wanted to waste police time on something that wasn't ever gonna happen, and I had to let him know that we didn't send squads chasing after every elf in the bushes, metaphorically speaking.

But then on the other hand, they teach you at the academy to listen to these nuts on the offsides that even nuts sometimes know something what might be true.

So I got to thinking I had this guy figured out, so I leaned forward and I said, "Pop, I know it's tough when families don't get along, and it ain't fair your daughter keeping you away from your grandson, but you know, the kid ain't gonna hold it against you if you get a friend to bring him his toys this year. The kid is gonna be a might upset if his mom takes out the deer rifle and pops you one. I mean if those're your options, you gotta know which one I recommend."

He got up and his voice went all deep, just like I was thinking it shoulda been, except it still wasn't jolly, and he said, "I *hate* going to the established authorities. They never believe me. Why can't you people have an open mind for once?"

The dispatch, he looked up from his nails, and the desk sarge who had come back in from wherever the hell he'd been looked at the old guy throw a fit right in front of me, a very cultured fit, but a fit all the same, and I knew what the sarge was thinking, he was thinking there goes Mantino again, pissing off some citizen.

I'd already heard the lecture about my melancholy state, about the way I should maybe get some help now that Cindy Lou was gone, only the lecture probably wouldn't go that way. It probably would be a bit harsher since Cindy Lou'd been gone nearly six months and my mood hadn't improved much. It was that empty house, you know, the starter, with two bedrooms the size of a closet, and the one empty as a grave, what was supposed to be for the first little Mantino way back when me and Cindy Lou actually liked each other. I'd been spending those last six months thinking, not about Cindy Lou because me and her we weren't right, but about family and how some people want one and never get it and how some people get one and never want it.

All this went through my brain in like a split second, while the geezer's using his elegant voice to broadcast to the whole house how I failed him. So I got up, and I said, not so loud that the sarge could hear, but loud enough to shut up the geezer, "If you got the magic that can make reindeer fly, how come you can't land on a roof without some wacko with a shotgun seeing you?"

The geezer sighed and got back in his chair. The desk sarge looked down, the dispatch went back to his nails, and all was right with the world.

Momentarily.

"The magic works like this," the geezer said. "Anyone who believes in me can see me."

I said, "Look, from what I can see in them letters, she don't believe in you."

"You haven't read closely enough," the old man said. "She believes strongly enough to see me as a threat to the entire civilized world. Unfortunately, she is probably the person who believes in me the most of all the adults in all the world."

He had a point. He had a delusion, she had a delusion, and it was shared and there was a gun mentioned, and I probably shoulda been taking this whole thing a lot more seriously than I had been.

"Okay," I said. "Whatta you want me to do?"

"I want you to go see her," he said, "and make her promise not to shoot me tomorrow night."

"You think that much hate is going to keep a promise?" I ask.

"She's a fanatic, isn't she?" he said. "She should keep a holy vow."

Right. Like I could extract a holy vow from a woman who hated Santa Claus. But it wasn't the hardest thing I'd ever had to do on this job.

So like an idiot, I agreed.

***

CHRISTMAS EVE, MY SHIFT started at noon, and since I didn't have a family, I was thinking maybe I'd work late, and then pick up some hours Christmas Day. I wasn't lying to myself that one day was like another; I knew

Christmas was special. I just figured if I worked through it, I wouldn't notice.

When I was a kid, the festivities started with the whole advent season. The second the decorations went up in church, they'd go up at home. My mom did the advent calendars and the whole nine yards, and it made December something else. I'd felt the lack ever since I moved from home—it wasn't the same after I'd left, and it got worse after she died—but it was never so bad as on Christmas and Christmas Eve.

I probably shoulda gone to midnight mass. I had it in my head I'd do it when I got off work, but I wasn't sure I wanted to see all them folks and their families in the red velvet and the fake fur coats, and me coming in in my uniform. I didn't figure it'd look right, you know?

And that's what I was trying not to think about as I drove up to this Prudence Billings' house. She lived in one of them ritzy areas of town—you know, those colonial houses with the columns and the eight miles of lawn before you even get to the front door. Santa had not just his choice of roofs, but he had his choice of chimneys here.

I didn't like her even worse than I didn't like her before, and that was before I got outta the squad.

I walked up that long sidewalk alone, noting that whoever shoveled didn't do a fine job as there was still a thin layer of ice that cracked beneath my boots. Someone had salted the steps, and the salt had melted through the ice, but no one'd bothered to kick the ice away, which I did, just as a courtesy.

Then I rang the bell.

The door opened and there was this kid wearing a pair of red shorts and a Santa hat, and grinning like there was no tomorrow. In that face, I saw every devil that ever walked and I knew that the geezer lied.

This kid wasn't good, he was hell on wheels, and I was just about to give him flight.

I caught him with one arm as he was about to sail into the snowy depths of the yard.

"Hey, kiddo," I said. "You ain't dressed for winter."

"Don't care," he said, struggling against me.

I wrapped my arm around him, lifted him off the ground and stepped inside with him. The hallway was one of them all wood jobbies with a staircase going up the side. The banister was covered in pine boughs, and there were ornaments hanging every which way.

"Miles?" a woman's voice shouted from above.

"He's down here," I said, hoping I didn't give her too much of a start. "I caught him going out the door."

I heard someone running across the floor upstairs, and then this girl peeked around the banister. Only it took me a half second to realize that wasn't no girl. That was a woman about my age who managed not only to keep her figure, but to keep lines off her face as well. Only her eyes told me she'd seen more of the world than any twenty-year-old ever could.

"And you are?" she asked, like someone in a uniform stood in her entry every day of the week.

"Name's Mantino, ma'am," I said with as much dignity as a man could muster when a three-year-old was squirming over his left arm, and kicking him perilously close to his private parts. "I'm with the police."

"I would hope so," she said. "Would you mind closing the door? It's got to be at least 20 degrees out there."

"Eighteen, ma'am," I said mostly because she had me a bit flustered. I didn't expect a person named Prudence Billings to look like this, kinda like a ballet dancer only without the ugly feet.

"Miles," she said, "where did you get that hat?"

The kid froze like he'd been dipped in ice, and truth be told, I kinda did too. I only heard one other woman on earth use that tone, and it was my mother back when I knew she'd caught me at something but good. My backside was twitching, and I would wager Miles's was too.

Still, he lifted his head over my bicep and grinned that Ain't-I-Cute? grin. "Got it at school," he said.

"Well, take it off," she said. "You know we don't allow that rubbish in here."

"Ma—"

"Miles."

He looked up at me and whispered, "Sorry but I gotta go now," and squirmed his way outta my arm. Then he tossed the hat at me like I gave it to him, and took off like a bat outta hell in the opposite direction. From that way, I smelled Christmas cookies, so I was wagering he was off to the kitchen to torment some poor housekeeper.

The lady sighed and came down the stairs. She was barefoot like I said, and her toenails were painted red and green and decorated with sprinkles that accent the colors. When she stopped on the landing, I noticed she wasn't quite as tall as I was. I figured when she was standing flat-foot on the floor she wasn't even gonna come up to my shoulders.

"What can I do for you, officer?"

I was twisting the red hat around in my hands like it was mine. She held out her hand for it, and I gave it to her. Her fingernails were long and painted just the same way. She didn't wear any rings.

"Prudence Billings?"

"Yes," she said.

I glanced at the hallway, lowered my voice, and then said, "I got some geezer come to the stationhouse last night saying you've been threatening Santa Claus."

She laughed. The sound was like a series of bells ringing on a starry night. "I have been."

I nearly took off my hat and started twisting it in my hands. "You said if he landed on your roof, you'd take a shotgun after him?"

"I said it to anyone who'd listen, Officer."

"Did you mean it?"

She looked at me, and I got the sense that this woman didn't do nothing she didn't mean. "Why do you ask?"

"Like I said, we gotta complaint—"

"Yes, I know. But not many folks would follow up on it. After all, my threat is only good if some man dressed in a red suit has his flying reindeer land a sleigh on my roof. In fact, I won't really do anything unless he slides down my chimney. I don't plan to sit on the lawn with the gun in my lap."

"Good thing," I said, "since it ain't something the neighbors would appreciate."

She laughed even though I was serious. So I got just a tad more serious.

"You gotta license for that shotgun?"

Her smile didn't just fade, it vanished like it never was, and I knew I had a lady who knew nothing about guns at all. A lady, a gun, and a kid. I didn't like how this was shaping up.

"'Fraid you gotta give it to me." I figured I'd keep it for the next few days, and the geezer wouldn't got nothing to worry about. By then maybe she'd rethink the whole gun-owning business. And if she didn't I'd give her a stern lecture when I got back on gun responsibility.

She stood on the landing, and said, "If you take the gun, will you protect me?"

"Seems to me that's a husband's job, ma'am," I said.

She looked up at me, and anger flared in her pretty eyes. I kinda liked the spark.

"Well, seeing as I don't have a husband, I'm relying on either myself or the police for protection."

"Protection from what, ma'am?"

"Santa Claus."

I sighed. I couldn't help it. "You know, ma'am, seems to me there's a lot more to worry about in this world than a man in a red suit who lands on your roof."

"You don't see it my way."

"No, ma'am. I always thought Santa was one of those guys who brought a little joy in the world, if you know what

I mean, ma'am." I was treading lightly here because while this broad was one of the most beautiful creatures I'd ever seen, she was probably some religious nut, and I wasn't in the mood to argue the religious implications of jolly ole St. Nick.

"He doesn't always bring joy," she said.

"No, he don't. Sometimes he misses kids. But the fire department and us, we do what we can to make sure them kids get something."

"To keep up the myth." Her voice was rising. I knew then I'd made some kinda mistake.

"Well, you know, it's kinda nice to have something to believe in." Then I winced, thinking she'd launch into the Jesus lecture, you know, the putting Christ back into Christmas thingie.

"No, it's not," she said, and I looked at her. I mean really looked at her.

This lady was scared.

So I said, "Tell me why you're doing this. It ain't natural to have something against Santa Claus."

"I'm trying to protect my son."

She *was* a loony. I sorta let the sigh out this time. "Lady, Santa leaves presents. I ain't never once heard a story where he traded 'em for the kids."

"That's not it," she said. "You saw him." And at first, I'm thinking she meant Santa Claus. Then I realize she meant the kid.

"Yeah," I said. "He's a pistol."

"Exactly." She came the rest of the way down the stairs and I was right. She didn't come up to my shoulders. But she smelled like roses, all delicate and fragile. "Miles is just like my brother."

"Is that a good thing, ma'am?"

"Not in this case. You're new to town, aren't you, officer?"

"Been here more'n two years, ma'am."

She shook her head. "When he was little, my brother fell off that roof and died. Broke his neck, which was probably for the best or so they tell me, since we didn't find him until Christmas morning. By then he was frozen stiff."

I didn't like how this was going. "I'm sorry to hear it, ma'am."

"He was seven. He was up there to watch Santa land." She swallowed. "My son is just like him. I don't want him to get wrapped up in the Santa myth. I'm afraid he'll do the same thing, and then I'll lose him too."

Her voice broke a little, and I put a hand on her shoulder. She didn't seem to mind.

"Look, ma'am," I said, feeling for her, knowing that we all go a little crazy over the things that hurt us most. "Your son ain't your brother—"

"I know," she said, "but I worry. And I think the best thing is to let him know that Santa isn't real, so then he'll avoid the whole thing. And he would be able to if the town didn't buy into this. I tried to prevent them from doing so, but it didn't work. Everyone still talks about Santa, and you've seen what it does to my son. He's got his Santa hat, and he's ready to show me that I'm wrong."

"Well, I think you are, ma'am," I said. "Santa ain't about materialism, not really, if you think about it. He's kinda a cherished cultural whatchamacallit—"

"Icon," she said.

"Yeah, whatever," I said. "He's one of them. Not because he brings us stuff, but because we think he does." That didn't come out the way I wanted it to so I took a deep breath and started over. "What I'm trying to say is this guy is okay to believe in because he's like pure good, you know. How many other examples do we got of someone who spends his whole year making stuff for others, then gives it all away in one night—to everyone, no one left out?"

"That's not how it works."

"Ain't it?" I said. "I been on various police forces for the last twenty years, and in all that time, I never seen a kid get missed by Santa, even if the Santa was a Toys for Tots program."

"If Santa was real," she said, "my brother wouldn't be dead."

"Ah, lady." I wanted to crouch down, face her at eye level and talk to her like a kid, because that's what she was sounding like. Some little teeny kid. "How old was you when all this came down?"

"Three," she whispered.

You didn't have to be no rocket scientist to figure out who she was protecting here, and it wasn't that underage demon in the red pants munchin' cookies in the kitchen.

"Look," I said, "You give me your shotgun, and I'll come back here when I'm off duty. I'll make sure Miles stays in his room, and Santa stays outside."

She raised her head. Her eyes were wide, and I thought I'd never seen anything so pretty in my whole life.

"You'd do that?" she asked. "Why?"

"Let's just say I think every kid needs a little guaranteed joy once a year, and three's too young to have it snatched away from you. Besides," I smiled at her. "I met your kid. He seems to me to be the type who'd go to the roof to prove to you that Santa *does* exist."

"I've been worried about that," she said. "I just hoped if I talked about it enough, the whole town would forget about this nonsense."

"It ain't nonsense, and no one'll forget," I said. "We all remember what it's like to be a kid and having that hope on Christmas Eve. We ain't gonna give it up, and we ain't gonna deny our kids the same thing."

"Do you have kids, officer?" she asked.

"I ain't found the right woman to have them with," I said.

She put a small hand on the side of my face. "Some woman doesn't know what she's missing," she said. Then she went upstairs, and brought me the gun.

***

I worked my regular shift, got off around eight, and flew outta the stationhouse. The dispatch, he made some crack about me having a date, and the whole group laughed like it wasn't possible, but I didn't say nothing. I just drove to the Billings place, hoping I wasn't too early. As it was, they was waiting for me.

Prudence Billings opened the door when I pulled up out front and motioned me inside. The pistol was wearing feet pajamas and his Santa cap, and holding a plate of cookies. I was thinking this kid wasn't gonna sleep for two weeks, judging by the brightness in his eyes.

"Miz Billings?" I'd changed into jeans and my heavy winter coat, figuring I was spending the night outside, waiting for the jingle of tiny sleigh bells.

"Priddy," she said.

"Ah, beg pardon?"

"Call me Priddy," she said. "Everyone does." Then she grinned. "It's better than Prude."

"Much," I said, thinking it seemed more accurate too. The house was looking nice. There was a tree in the living room, and white lights on the evergreen boughs on the stairs. The place was fairly bursting to be festive, and I figured it wouldn't take a lot of work to get Priddy Billings to start celebrating in a way that'd satisfy the kid.

"I got cookies for you, Mister," the pistol said.

"Thanks," I said, and took one. It was a sugar cookie with a bit too much frosting, but it had a sweet lemony taste like the ones my mom used to make. The taste of Christmas, sure as I breathed.

"It's officer," Priddy was saying to the kid. "Officer Mantino."

"Actually," I said, "it's Nick."

She grinned. "How appropriate," she said.

I guess it was. I never thought of it that way. "Well," I said, "what's the plan?"

"The plan is to get Miles to bed, and then I'll hold down the inside while you guard the outside."

"Seems fair," I said. "You ready to sleep, sport?"

"I'm not gonna sleep," he said. "I'm gonna show Mom that Santa's coming."

Priddy closed her pretty eyes.

"Well," I said, crouching down to be at his level. "You ain't gonna do that by staying awake."

"Why not?" the kid asked.

"You don't know?" I said. "Santa don't come to houses where kids are awake."

I thought Priddy's mouth was gonna fall off her face. I guess she hadn't thought of that one. It was a simple solution to her problem. Keep the kid awake all night and Santa wouldn't show up. Too late now. I'd spilled the beans.

"That true?" the kid asked.

"Scouts honor," I said, holding up my hand.

"You was a scout?" he asked.

"Eagle," I said, not lying.

"Wow," he said. "You know, I wanna be a scout."

"*Miles,*" Priddy said in that voice again.

"Ah, Mom," he said, but started up the stairs anyway. Halfway up, he stopped. "You wanna read to me, Mister?"

"Officer Mantino has done enough." Priddy marched past me and went with the kid. "He'll be guarding the house tonight, so you say thank you."

"Thank you," the kid said. "Merry Christmas."

That last was a little forlorn, so I grinned at him. "Merry Christmas, sport."

Then he trudged the rest of the way up the stairs. She followed. I wandered into the living room, wondering if she really wanted me to snoop that far into their lives. The tree was big and green and smelled like pine heaven. Under it were more presents than I'd received since I'd grown up, all in that shiny wrapping paper that reflected the lights.

The lady wasn't loony. She was just fighting something she shoulda dealt with long ago. She'd mixed up believing in Santa with the death of her brother, and then with the growing up of her kid. I was really glad now I got the shotgun outta the house. I wasn't looking forward to a night in the snow, but I figured it was a small price to pay for what I hoped was a chance to take Priddy Billings to dinner—when the holidays was over and she turned back into a normal person again.

It took her a while, but she finally came down the stairs. I was back in the hallway by then. She put a finger to her lips and led me into the kitchen. In there, I saw the remains of a Christmas ham. She handed me a bag filled with sandwiches and a thermos of coffee.

"Sorry to send you out on a night like this."

I shrugged. It wasn't a bad night. Just cold. "I volunteered."

"You're a nice man," she said.

"I got my moments."

"You think I'm crazy, don't you?"

That's one of them trick questions. If I said yes, I doomed this friendship for life. If I said no, I'd be lying. "I think you got issues," I said.

"You're polite too," she said.

I set the bag and the thermos on the table, then pulled my gloves outta my pocket and put my wool cap over my ears. "I'd better get out there."

"You think he'll come this early?"

"Priddy." I liked the way the name sounded when I said it. "I don't think he'll come at all, but I think we should be vigilant now, just in case."

"Good point," she said, and went back upstairs. She stopped at the kitchen door. "Thank you, Nick."

"You're welcome," I said, and let myself out the back.

***

I wasn't gonna hide. I thought the worst thing I could do was wedge myself behind some bush and freeze to death, making Priddy relive her Christmas horror, and giving the kid a bad fright too. I had this all figured. In my car were a few things that a sales clerk assured me a three-year-old boy would like. I was gonna give 'em to Priddy around dawn, before the kid was up. I figured it was up to her to say whether the stuff came from me, a stranger, or Santa, a made-up stranger.

Maybe by then, she'd be willing to acknowledge Santa. If we made it through the night without him, that is. And I figured we would. First, you know, adult common sense said there was no such thing as Santa. But if there was, no self-respecting Santa would show up when people were looking for him. But I did figure there was a chance the geezer would come, and I kinda wanted to head him off at the pass. Maybe sometime in the next year, him and Priddy would resolve whatever differences they had. Maybe I'd still be around to help 'em do it.

So that's what I was thinking. I trudged around the yard, wearing a hole in the snow that probably wasn't doing the lawn any good. I watched the neighbors lights go out one by one, and I sucked down too much coffee and had to wait until one whole side of the neighborhood was dark before getting rid of some of it.

I think it was long about one a.m. when I got the bright idea to get the ice off Priddy's sidewalk. It was too late to use a shovel—that scrape-scrape-scrape would wake up the dead—so I decided to use my boot.

I was working my way from the porch to the road when I saw something move on the roof. I let out a four-banger blue alarm cuss that woulda sent me packing if Priddy heard it, and stepped back for a better look.

Damned if the geezer wasn't there, in his red suit and red hat, and looking jolly. Behind him was reindeer—at least some kinda deer—hooked onto a sleigh that was made of dark wood with red trim. It had curled runners, and the back end was piled high with toy sacks.

The geezer held up his mittened hand and waved at me. Then he hoisted himself onto the chimney, and I started cussing again. I mean, what was I gonna do to stop him, pelt him with snowballs? By the time I got to the back door, the geezer'd disappeared through the chimney and I was praying to every god I could think of that Priddy hadn't hid another weapon where I couldn't see it.

I slid through the back door, and tracked sludge on the linoleum. I slammed open the swinging doors, hurried through the decorated hallway, and stopped in the living room.

There he was, crouched beside the tree, laying train tracks—bright yellow and blue PlaySkool® train tracks with a big fat engine just perfect for a three-year-old. He set a kid-sized basketball hoop on the antique chair beside the fireplace, and put a small basketball beneath it. Then he turned around and pointed at me.

"I expect you to make sure he uses this," the geezer said in that prim tone of his.

"Me?" I said, looking behind me, thinking maybe Priddy was there. But she wasn't. I could hear her light step on the floor above. "Hey, you didn't tell me the whole story."

"But I do want to thank you," the geezer said. "I didn't see a shotgun."

"I got the shotgun," I said. "But she has a legitimate gripe. Her brother died on Christmas Eve. He fell off the roof. You got magic. How come you didn't do nothing?"

The jolly left the geezer's face. Suddenly it was like he was eighty years older than he'd been before.

"Magic has limitations," he said. "Mine is limited to this kind of joyfulness. Do you know how many little children ask me to get their mommies and daddies back together or to put an end to war? I can't. I don't have the power."

"You got the power to grab some kid who's sliding off a roof," I said, and there was a bit of force behind my words. You know, if this guy was who he said he was—and he had to be, didn't he?, I seen the deer—then I'd been idolizing him for some time. I coulda caught a kid with one hand, and pulled him to safety. This geezer coulda too.

"No, I don't," he said. "And you know why."

"The hell I do," I said.

He squinted at me.

"Because," he said, "I don't come to houses where people are awake."

"I'm awake."

"Yes, I know," he said. "But I asked you for help. It's a slightly different circumstance. And I wouldn't be here if Miles weren't sleeping. Soundly."

"So you didn't come at all that night, the night the kid died?"

"Ask Miss Billings," the geezer said, looking over my shoulder.

I turned. She was behind me, looking small. Her eyes were bright with unspent tears. They reflected the tree lights.

"You didn't come, did you?" she said in that little kid voice. "There were no special presents under the tree. I remember now. I hadn't thought of that. It hadn't seemed like Christmas that day. You didn't come because I was awake. I was waiting for my brother to come back to bed. Oh, God," she said, and her voice broke. "I killed him."

"No," I said.

"No," the geezer said at the same time. Only he went on. "It was one of those things that magic doesn't have a solution to. I'm so very sorry."

We were silent for what seemed like forever, waiting to see what Priddy would do. Finally, she blinked and one of the tears fell. Then she looked at the tree.

"Are those for Miles?" she asked.

"Yes," the geezer said.

"Wait," she said, and disappeared around the corner. I was hoping that she didn't go to do something stupid, but I didn't stop her. It was between her and the geezer now.

"You coulda told me," I said.

"You had to discover it for yourself," the geezer said.

"Why?" I ask.

He smiled. "Because I can't do anything without making a gift out of it."

"A gift?" I say.

He nodded, and then Priddy came back into the room. She was carrying that plate of cookies that Miles had out for me, and a glass of milk.

"We need to follow the tradition," she said.

The geezer took one of the cookies, and ate it. He grabbed the rest of the cookies and shoved them in his pocket—"for the reindeer," he said around the food—all except one, a Santa whose red suit was a bit too pink. He bit the head off it, and left it and a bunch of crumbs on the plate. "A tradition," he said and swallowed. He took the milk from Priddy, drank it all, and handed her the glass back. His mustache was dripping.

He looked at Priddy. "I'm glad this is finally settled."

"Between us it's settled," she said. "But it'll never be all right."

That sad look was back on his face. "My dear, things like this are never all right. But we do learn how to go on living, despite the pain."

"I guess we do," she said.

Then he smiled at her. "There is a gift for you here, too," he said. "If you only see it."

She looked at the tree. I was watching him. He put a finger alongside his nose, gave me a nod—and just like in the damn poem—up the chimney he rose.

Priddy looked back at me.

"He's gone," she said.

"Yep," I said. Then I cleared my throat. "I guess you won't be needing me no more."

She put a hand on my arm. "It was kind of you to give up your family time to help us."

I shrugged. "Ain't got family no more, ma'am. So it was no bother at all."

She looked at me, like she was seeing me for the first time. "Then I insist you stay. We have a guest room, and a Christmas turkey that's too big for Miles and me."

"I couldn't," I said. "It's a family day."

"It's no bother," she said. "Really. You helped us. I'd like to repay you." Then I grinned. She meant it. She really did. "I got stuff for Miles in the car."

"You were going to be Santa," she said.

"I think it's important," I said.

She glanced at the chimney.

"I guess it's important," she said, "even when we don't admit it."

"Especially then," I said.

***

Now I wouldn'ta told you all this except in the context that we been discussing nutcases. You see, the next morning, over Priddy's protests, I went out on that roof, and there weren't no sleigh marks or footprints or hoof prints. There wasn't no soot on Priddy's polished floor neither, and later I found a receipt for one basketball hoop, child-sized, by the cookie jar in the pantry.

I woulda thought Priddy was humbugging us all with them threats while celebrating like everyone else did if I hadn't come down with a humdinger of a cold from standing outside for too long on an icy December night. Priddy brought me her housekeeper's famous chicken soup and she took care of me during that awful week.

We've become something of a thing, you know, me and Priddy, and the guys at the stationhouse think it's funny; some woman from old money hooking up with a guy like me. But they don't know that we have lots to share, her and me. I'm the one who believes in stuff; she's the one who needs to. She's the one with the family; I'm the one who needs one. Stuff like that.

We're gonna make it official next Christmas season, but we're getting a new house. Something between my starter and her colonial, something that's just ours. It'll have a roof, but nothing too high, so if the kid gets adventurous—and he won't, not while I'm around—he won't get killed if he slips off.

I just keep thinking about the geezer, you know? I keep thinking maybe we should invite him to the wedding. After all, he's the one what brought us together. And I wonder if we send a wedding invite to that North Pole address the kids use, if he'll get it, and if he gets it, will he show?

Then I think about what I'm worrying about, and I check to see if it's a full moon or something. You know. Nutball season.

Because there's a part of me that's still embarrassed I believe in the old guy, even though I do. Since he was right. He gave all three of us a gift that night.

He gave the kid Christmas and he gave me and Priddy each other.

And that's enough to make anyone believe in Santa—even nutballs. Like me.

About the Author

INTERNATIONAL BESTSELLING WRITER Kristine Kathryn Rusch has published fiction in every genre. She has been nominated for three Edgar Awards, two Shamus Awards, and an Anthony Award. She has won the *Ellery Queen* Reader's Choice Award twice. She has also won two Hugo awards, a World Fantasy Award, and three *Asimov's* Readers Choice Awards. She writes mystery as Kris Nelscott, paranormal romance as Kristine Grayson, as well as the science fiction and fantasy that she's known for under Rusch. For more information about her work, please go to kristinekathrynrusch.com.

Also by
Kristine Kathryn Rusch

The Retrieval Artist Series:

The Disappeared
Extremes
Consequences
Buried Deep
Paloma
Recovery Man
Duplicate Effort
Anniversary Day
Blowback

The Smokey Dalton Series (as Kris Nelscott):

A Dangerous Road
Smoke-Filled Rooms
Thin Walls
Stone Cribs
War at Home
Days of Rage

WMG
Publishing